Blind Revenge

Blind Revenge

(Jim Cobb Mystery #2)

by
Mike Nails

Hybrid Global Publishing

Blind Revenge
Published by Hybrid Global Publishing Tel: (646) 232-9647

hybridglobalpublishing.com
ISBN 978-1-961757-51-6

To my Brothers
Jerry Adams, Mark Banks, Lowell Gephert, Rick Renardson,
Rob Spence, and Terry West.
All part of the 3RD Surgical Hospital, Can Tho,
Viet Nam 1969-70.

Whoever fights monsters should see to it that in the process he does not become a monster.

And if you gaze long enough into an abyss, the abyss will gaze back into you.

— Friedrich Nietzsche

Blind Revenge

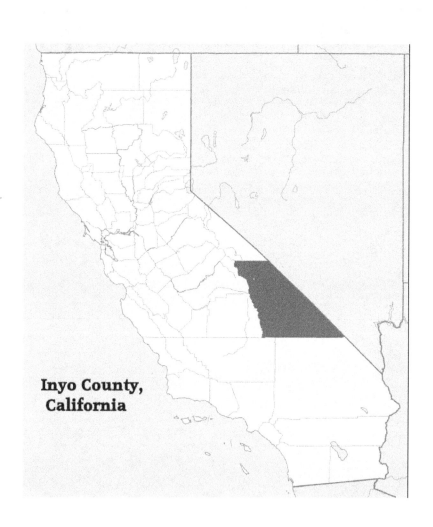

Inyo County, California

Chapter 1

S ix weeks after the surprise attack on Pearl Harbor, Wally Snyder, a wiry, six-foot, brown-eyed and curly brown-haired patriot, took a sip of the last of his morning coffee inside the hidden cave where he had slept the night before.

The eighteen-year-old cowboy was enjoying one last camping trip before starting basic training and shipping out with the Army in three weeks. His campsite was inside a cave with a rock overhang, halfway up the side of a mountain overlooking Death Valley. The secluded location hid him from anybody looking up from the valley floor. His dark bay-colored mustang, tethered in the back of the cave, whinnied. The remnants of a small mesquite fire released a whiff of telltale smoke, which dispersed into the mountain air.

The high desert was desolate, not another human being in sight for miles. He wanted the lonely emptiness one last time before boarding a bus, headed for basic training at Ford Ord in Monterey County.

Wally liked to come out, alone, to the valley and camp. The freedom to do what he wanted, without getting permission from his father or older brother. Enlisting in the Army was the first decision he'd made as an adult. It was the right thing to do. A foreign country, Japan, had attacked the U.S. Navy at Pearl Harbor without provocation. It was a sucker punch to the gut of America, unwarranted and without merit.

Wally—who'd just graduated from high school the past June—had never participated in a fight growing up. He didn't know of anyone who didn't like him, and for the life of him could never get his head around a motive the Japanese could give for the surprise attack. Wally never talked with anyone about his lack of understanding as to why one country attacked another. Last night, sleeping in the cavern, he'd wished he had a girlfriend he could have shared his thoughts, dreams, and aspirations with.

Someone to listen to what he wanted to do with his life, the kind of man he wanted to ultimately become—a husband, father, and pillar of the community.

In three weeks, he would be learning what it takes to kill the enemy—with no close friends or even a girlfriend to miss him. Before the attack, Wally had been happy to work with his father on the family's cattle ranch, see a movie with his brother, and dream of what life could bring him. Now, the Army owned him, lock, stock, and barrel.

Facing Wally's camp, high up the mountainside above Furnace Creek, the morning sun was just above the rim of the mountains across the valley floor. The night temperature had fallen below forty degrees, and the expected high for the coming day was eighty-six. The few wisps of thin, milky white clouds off to the north would melt away over the next two hours. The air was clean, the sky endless, and the desert floor alive with its natural inhabitants—birds, insects, reptiles, and the occasional mouse or rabbit destined to be dinner for an ever-present predator. Raw nature excited the young man, survival, eat or be eaten, always keeping one eye open, never taking anything for granted.

Ten a.m. rolled around. Wally cleaned up the cave, packing away a canvas bag with anything he couldn't stuff in his saddlebags, and dispersing the remains of his morning fire. He threw a saddle cloth over his horse's back, put the saddle on, and cinched up the leather belt under his belly; then repeated the effort after Lookout, his horse, let out a breath—the mechanics of preparing his horse and getting ready to return home.

Wally was leading his horse to the mouth of the cave when he heard the noise of several large trucks coming up from the valley floor. He rubbed the face of his mustang horse. Wally and his father had rounded up twenty wild horses three years earlier. After breaking this particular young horse, Wally named him Lookout. The colt whinnied and shook his head up and down in appreciation for the attention his master was showing. He tied his horse to a sizable rock away from the opening, took off his hat, and belly crawled out of the cave to the ledge overlooking the area below. He kept himself out of sight until he reached the edge in front of the cave. The tableland was fifteen feet from the mouth of the cave to the sheer drop-off. There was nothing between the edge and valley floor two-hundred feet below.

Eight Studebaker two-and-a-half-ton military cargo trucks and a Willys MB quarter-ton US Army Jeep drove up in a single file and stopped. Soldiers emerged from the truck cabs and covered backs, with their rifles at the ready. Wally counted a total of twenty soldiers. He couldn't take his eyes off the gathering below: who were these soldiers, where did they come from, why were they here in Death Valley, what were their orders, and how were these soldiers going to carry out the orders given?

Wally's questions started to develop into answers. People—no, they were all male; short and slight in stature and of all ages, from teenage boys to old men, were taken from the back of each truck. They all wore thin shirts and pants, but no hats, and had their hands tied behind their backs with rope. All were led to a massive open trench cut into the ground directly below Wally's position outside the cave. The trench appeared machine-dug, but any equipment used was no longer on site. He guessed the opening in the valley floor was roughly fifteen feet wide, fifty feet long, and close to twenty or more feet deep.

The first group of men, thirty-two in all, were placed in front of the trench. All facing out across the valley floor and away from the cave. The rest of the prisoners remained near the trucks with guards, while sixteen soldiers stood ten to twelve feet behind the tied-up men. A separate man, who was in command, ordered the armed men to raise their weapons and fire.

An ear-splitting report rose from the killing field, causing Wally to hunker down into the dirt with his arms over his head. Lookout whinnied, trying to free himself.

After the sound passed, Wally raised his face to look over the rim. Each shot prisoner now lay on the ground, face down, before the trench. The man who gave the command gave a second command to fire at the remaining seven or eight still standing prisoners. Two men walked behind shooting a single bullet into the back of the head of each man, most likely using a 1911 Colt .45, and reloading with a new clip before reaching the end of the line. Two soldiers came up and dragged the bodies to the edge of the trench, throwing them into the chasm below. Taking shovels from the trucks, and using the mound of dirt on the far side of the trench, they covered the evidence of the executions.

Wally vomited after seeing the unadulterated slaughter. He used water from his canteen to wash his face and mouth, then sat down in the cave next to his horse, holding Lookout's head as the horse nudged him. He was horrified by the brutality he witnessed—the callous disregard for life—whoever those men were, no one deserved to die in such a manner.

Shaking and sweating from the ordeal, Wally led his horse out of the cave, mounted, and rode away up the mountain to a gap between two peaks. He was traveling home to Owens Valley. He needed to get home before nightfall, or his dad would worry. Wally didn't know that four more executions, like the one he witnessed, would take place on this day, leading to 161 unfortunate executed bodies filling the trench in Death Valley.

The extermination completed, the soldiers boarded the trucks, turned the vehicles, and headed back the way they came. The Jeep remained, the two men who shot the prisoners in the head sitting in the back of the Jeep. In the passenger seat sat another man next to the driver. Both of these men looked like officers.

When he was leaving, Wally hadn't noticed that the Jeep was still on the valley floor, but the man in the passenger seat, First Sergeant Wade Arnold, did see the lone rider leave the hidden cave on his horse. Arnold was a twenty-five-year-old, six-foot, barrel-chested man with a mean hatchet face. His childhood had been lived in the high desert, under the heavy hand of a drunken father. They had scratched out a meager existence from sunup to sunset on ranch land too barren to even raise one head of cattle, let alone a herd.

His mother had left the family when he was seven years old. Just before he turned sixteen, he'd run away from home and had a hard-luck life until finding himself at the Hayes Date Ranch in Indian Wells down in Riverside County. Since then, he had worked on the date ranch, where he had become best friends with Jamison Hayes. He had even followed Jamison into the Army.

The lone rider's destination could only be Owens Valley. Wade Arnold knew he would have to find the intruder, the sole witness to the extermination performed by his commanding officer for God and Country.

The execution in Death Valley was clandestine, off the books; no one else knew of its existence. The officer, now Captain Jamison Hayes, a rock-ribbed man of six feet in height with broad shoulders, and crisp creases in his uniform, wanted the mission done to avenge the deaths of all who had perished in Pearl Harbor. Arnold was a little shorter than Captain Hayes, and did anything that Hayes wanted to be done, never questioning or thinking of the consequences. He had blind faith in the orders of his commanding officer. Everything was right with the world as long as they kept the status quo.

The only thought rushing through First Sergeant Arnold's mind was finding the cowboy riding toward Owens Valley. If word got out about what transpired on this day, all hell would break out.

Chapter 2

It was an uneventful Tuesday afternoon in January 1962, when I received a call from my wife, Conchita. She had just returned from the doctor's office with our littlest one, two-year-old Rosie, an equal representation of her mother, olive skin, eyes, and temperament. I know Rosie will be a handful when she finds out about boys; my only wish is I won't have to send her to a convent to relieve my anxieties.

Conchita wanted me to go over to the pharmacy in Lone Pine on the way home and pick up a prescription for liquid penicillin. Rosie has an ear infection again. I asked Conchita, 'How is everything else?'

With a smile in her voice, Conchita replied, 'My sister came by earlier, to take care of Gabe and Tom while I went to the doctor. They're both out back playing cowboys and indians right now.'

'At least they're not playing cops and robbers.' I thought about our twin boys. They had complete opposites features, with Tom more like my side of the family; taller, lean, with hazel eyes. Gabe, the apple of the eye of Conchita's family, was husky, with dark hair, black eyes, and ready to take on the world. Both boys, now four years old, are full of piss and vinegar, just like their grandfather Merrill, who is due to arrive from Mexico over the upcoming weekend.

My father had gone down to Zihuatanejo, a fishing village on the Mexican Pacific Coast north of Acapulco, right after New Year's in 1958, to live out his life. In his travels, he'd met Delfina Ruiz, a feisty, in-your-face woman. From the photos he sent us, Delfina is sultry, with dark skin and black almond eyes that seem to look right through you.

Dad says Delfina is the most giving individual he has ever met. 'There is nothing she would not do for you, and I mean nothing,' he wrote. Sounds like she's a pistol who keeps my father in line. She feeds him, cleans his clothes, and screws him in any room, on any surface, at any time either one wants. I still can't believe my father and Delfina are together.

She is the ideal foil for my dad. He is one lucky cowboy.

As I rolled each member of my family around in my head, I considered their pluses and minuses and realized that each one, warts and all, was the best the world could give. Life was good. Now I just needed to pick up the prescription for Rosie.

I went out to the lot and started up my new 1962 Dodge Dart 413-CID V8, a real muscle car. I left the Sheriff's office and headed to the Lone Pine Pharmacy.

The only customer was an older woman in the aisle that sold bath soaps and deodorant. I walked to the back and stood in front of the counter where Owen Snyder was working. He looked up.

'Hi, Owen. How is everything?'

'Good, Sheriff, excellent. I think you came in for a liquid penicillin prescription for your little girl.'

Smiling, I said, 'That's right.'

'Here it is.' As Owen held out a small white bag containing the prescription, he paused and glanced around. 'I have something I need to talk to you about, Jim.'

'Go ahead, what is it?'

Leaning forward, Owen said, 'My brother Wally is missing.'

I knew their parents had died in the early 1950s, Owen and Wally were the only family left. 'What do you mean by missing?'

'He called me last week. He said he needed to tell me something vital, that his life depended on the information,' Owen replied.

That piqued my curiosity. 'What is it?'

'I don't know, he never contacted me again.'

My mind jumped into sheriff's mode. 'Did you go out to where he lives?'

'Yes, I did, a couple of days ago. The trailer Wally lives in was locked up, and the truck he owns was gone. I talked with some of his neighbors and they have not seen him since a week ago.' Owen shrugged helplessly.

'Okay,' I paused, thinking. 'Does Wally have any friends he could have gone to?'

'No, Jim, Wally has been a loner since he returned from the war right after V-E Day.'

'Well, Owen, I'll call the office and get a deputy to try to find your brother. I need you to go in and fill out a missing person's report. Everything you can think of about Wally. Remember, adults can do whatever they want and not tell anyone.'

'Thanks, Sheriff.'

I turned to leave and thought of something. 'Owen, do you think Wally went out on a bender?'

'Jim, as far as I know, Wally hasn't had a drink for over eight months. But you never know, right?'

'Okay, Owen, I'll call the office. Thanks again for this. What do I owe you?' I said, holding up my little girl's prescription as I walked out of the pharmacy.

'Consider it payment for looking for Wally.'

Driving home, I thought about growing up with the Snyder boys. Owen was now average in height and complexion, with brown eyes and hair. We went to school together. He was the student who wanted to play sports but couldn't because he contracted polio when he was eight years old. He'd worn a brace on his right leg ever since.

The younger son by two years, Walter Snyder, known as Wally to everyone in the school, was full of laughs, always smiling, and a natural-born athlete. Wally, the all-American boy, tall, muscular, with baby blue eyes and blond hair. Whenever there was a pickup game at the sandlot, Wally refused to be on any team but Owen's. After high school graduation in June of 1941, Wally worked on the family ranch as a cowboy. He enlisted in the Army in late December, right after Pearl Harbor, leaving his father to work the small cattle ranch alone.

The Dodge Dart ran smoothly as I thought about life in my little corner of the world. Everything seemed as good as it could get. I was married to the best woman in the world, father of three children, and had a job I looked forward to each day.

Since the capture and death of the Hanging Murderer, Silas Reid, and the arrest of Barton Haskel's killer, Lottie Pilgrim, five years ago, Inyo County had returned to the sleepy, crime-free, peace-loving community I grew up in.

Finding Owen Snyder's younger brother didn't seem a severe problem to solve. I never liked anything I couldn't make sense of, whether or not Wally's disappearance fit the category was still to be seen.

Chapter 3

The scruffy-looking man in the 1940 Chevy truck had a two-day beard, wrinkled clothes, and a mean disposition. Since leaving Southern California five years earlier, he had killed more than twenty people, mostly women who were walking on roads alone, or were local prostitutes.

Once leaving the United States, the man worked his way down along the Sea of Cortez to the little pueblo of Puerto Peñasco, doing odd jobs, mostly menial labor. Just enough to pay for a roof over his head, some food, tequila, and a woman now and then. The man didn't need much to get by. He didn't want to be noticed, he loved invisibility. He was never the one at the front looking for notoriety.

After five years in Mexico, the new year began with some fireworks, copious amounts of tequila, and another young male who wanted him.

The man was reminded about the last time he was in Banning, California—the reason he had moved south to Mexico. A young man he'd picked up in the Chevy truck, who'd said he would do anything the man wanted. The man would fuck white, black, Indian, or Mexican women, but not a queer. He strangled the young man right after he got in the truck, and dumped the body immediately, without regard to location or time of day.

Gripping the steering wheel tightly, knuckles white, he couldn't think of anything else. A queer? In his vehicle? Never again. He was repulsed by the very thought. He strangled the kid and buried him in a shallow grave past the dunes, inland from the Sea of Cortez. The body was found no more than a couple of hours after the drop, and a sense of foreboding engulfed the man driving the truck.

The victim was a local kid who was known by many, including the Federales officials. The man from the truck found out that the dead boy was a younger brother of the Captain of the Federales.

This newest development, another killing, created a second look at Mexico as a safe place to live. A few days later, he drove north out of Puerto Peñasco to the United States. The date was January 4, 1962.

The windblown old Chevy truck, which had started out as a dark blue color so many years before, was now almost raw metal. The route north consisted of Mexico Rte. 3 to Rte. 40 and the border town of San Luis Los Olivos. Once on the American side, Yuma, Arizona, opened its arms and welcomed the man home. He stayed a couple of days before taking Arizona State Rte. 195 north to Rte. 95, until he reached US Route 66 and Kingman.

He knew a little red-haired woman he would stop by and see now and then back in the mid-1950s. He drove to the old cabin and saw three little ginger-headed kids playing in the yard among several old wrecks.

He stopped the truck and got out, keeping the door open, window down, and one foot on the running board, while waiting for the woman to come out of the cabin.

The red-haired woman came out holding a shotgun. Her hair was tangled and ratty looking. She was thinner and worn out from her life, caring for her unwanted children alone. Her blank expression changed to recognition after a minute or two. The three kids kept playing, not paying any attention to the man.

The woman lowered the shotgun, waving the man over to her. They looked at each other without interest, just recognition. She didn't have any other options for the day and remembered that he didn't beat her; he had even left her some money when he visited last.

They went inside and made their way to her bedroom. She didn't fix her hair or brush her teeth. An hour later, they lay on their backs amongst the sweat-soaked sheets, both physically spent. Before he rose to get dressed, she told him that the oldest child outside was his, she'd named him Toby. He was a good boy who minded his mom.

As the man walked outside, he took a long look at the oldest child. Shaking his head, he said to himself, *that bastard boy isn't mine, no matter what she says*. He knew this was the last time he would make a stop to see this woman. He got in his truck and left, looking for a Mexican place to eat.

There were thousands of venues in California, Nevada, and Arizona the man had visited over the last thirty years or so—some good, others not so good. They were all different, but there wasn't a single woman or house that stood out; the memories seemed to blend together.

The best part of driving on the highways and byways of the southwest was that when another road came up over the hill, no one told him which route to take. He was alone, without a single care in the world, just the way he wanted his life.

The man felt no despair in being alone, it was a life he had chosen without even thinking. His lifelong adage—of visitors and fish smelling after three days—keeping him safe from any lengthy stays.

The radio played a country melody by Patsy Cline, "*I Fall to Pieces*," the artist's number one hit of the previous year. He knew the song but steadfastly told himself that life was more significant than a mere song. Nothing and no one made this *hombre* fall to pieces.

Chapter 4

Edith Pearson has been my secretary since I was elected Sheriff in 1956. Before me, she had been secretary to my dad, Merrill, since the day she came to work in the Sheriff's department in May of 1948. Now thirty-seven, still single, independent, and always looking for a fun time, she was the full-time 'boss' of my office in Independence.

She'd had an affair for a couple of years with Barton Haskel after she began working for my dad. When the Hanging Murderer returned, she met up with a newspaper gossip writer who came to Lone Pine to do a story about a new Randolph Scott movie filmed the previous spring.

Edith had met Grady Bennett, the writer from the *LA Post*, at the Cowboy Bar and Grill. They'd started having an affair right before Barton Haskel's murder. I caught Barton's murderer, the story was dropped off the front page, and she was alone again.

The last five years had been lean for Edith's love life, but each year she did take vacation time and was able to go see other parts of the country—exciting places like Miami, New Orleans, and San Francisco.

As I entered my office, I called out, 'Edith, yesterday at the pharmacy, Owen Snyder told me his younger brother, Wally, is missing. Call up Owen and get all the particulars.'

'Jim, Owen came in early this morning, and already gave me the information.'

'Good news. What would I do without you, Edith?'

'You'll never find out because that will never happen,' Edith laughed as she glanced at me. 'I'm here for the rest of my days.'

'What if some strong man comes along and puts you on the back of his horse and wants you to ride away with him?' I asked.

'Jim, look around Inyo County,' Edith smiled as she shrugged, 'there aren't any single men in the area. I'd have to leave our beautiful community to find any action with an unknown fella.

That's what vacations are for. Anyway, the last *real* man was taken by Conchita Ramirez, if I'm not mistaken. How are your wife and kids today?'

'Well Edith, the boys are hellions, and Rosie has an earache. As for Conchita, she is the love of my life. She is...' Before I could finish my sentence, a stranger walked into the department.

He was at least six-feet-four, broad-shouldered, and rugged-looking, with stubble on his wind-burned face and held a worn Stetson in his hands in front of his chest. He looked out of place, like this was his first visit to the Sheriff's office. His dark brown eyes made him look like a puppy dog wanting a new owner. The stranger exhibited a warm, friendly, down-home feeling without saying a word.

Edith rose from her desk, straightened her dress, fluffed her hair, and smiled as she walked up to the stranger, and asked, 'Can I help you, sir?'

The man smiled as if for now, everything was right with the world. He said, 'Yes, Ma'am, I'm looking for the Sheriff. I want to report a murder.'

Chapter 5

Inyo County is rural, a couple of main highways, few secondary roads, and then there's the area where no paths exist. These no-road areas of the county require horse travel. Our destination was just such a place, beyond the primitive road signs.

Alex Morgan, a rancher from south of Owens Lake, came into my office on January 10, 1962, to report a murder. In my office, he'd told me that he'd found three dead—presumably soldiers—sitting in an army Jeep in a cave, just by chance, as he was hiking in the area of Malpais Mesa, a desolate area close to Death Valley. Alex said the inside of the cave was like a tomb, the air was dry, humidity zero, no moisture, and the skin on the deceased was like old, worn leather. He didn't touch anything and didn't look for a cause of death. The dead men were all dressed in fatigues, hats on, with a thin layer of dust covering everything.

I rode along with Deputy Perry Rimmer out to Morgan's ranch and helped him hitch up a trailer with three horses for the ride out to the Mesa.

January of 1962 was not a high crime time for Inyo County, and murder was low on our priorities, since the end of the Hanging Murderer and Barton Haskel's killer back in 1958. In other words, the peacekeeping work was slow.

Before leaving Independence, I told Perry to contact the FBI, and the U.S. Army Military Police at Fort Irwin, located in San Bernardino County.

Edith called the Adams Funeral Home in Lone Pine; the owner, Earl, worked with the county medical examiner's office in Los Angeles County and Coroner Dr. Mark Crawley.

Each organization was ordered to assemble at Alex Morgan's ranch. The narrow primitive road ran ten miles from Alex's ranch before becoming just a worn trail, only accessible by horse for the next twenty miles, to get to the cave with the bodies. But just past the cave, the track widened enough for the jeep to enter. Death Valley was farther to the east.

The group was told that the area of investigation was at Malpais Mesa. The inhospitable location had few visitors, and no one lived in the area. The perfect place to stash a few bodies never meant to be found.

Alex, Perry, and I would all be three to four hours ahead of the others. There was no need to rush. From what Alex described, the deceased had been in the cave since the Second World War.

Chapter 6

Perry, Alex, and I arrived in the early afternoon, after three hours of hard uphill riding for the horses. The location was hot and dry for early January; the temperature outside the cave was in the mid-60s. The location, high desert, had an abundance of Joshua trees and cactus, but little other vegetation.

Alex directed us down from the mesa into a small canyon; the mouth of the cave was hidden, the opening visible only after a sharp turn to the left. The inside of the cavern was bone-dry and at least thirty by thirty feet in width and depth, and twenty feet in height. The outside opening was roughly ten by ten feet, big enough for a military Jeep. The road the Jeep came in on went off to the east.

The Jeep was parked about twenty-five yards back from the opening, pointed toward the front portal, as if it had been backed in. There were no other tire tracks or footprints other than the ones Alex had created.

The three bodies were mummified, with dry, darkened skin. They all wore army field uniforms last used during the Second World War. All three were firmly tied to their seats with rope under their shirts, sitting stiffly upright, facing straight ahead.

The manufacturer's plate for the vehicle was stamped on the driver-side opening—Willys MA model, US Army Jeep, assembled in Toledo, Ohio, November 1940. The four-wheel-drive utility vehicle looked almost brand new, with hardly any wear. The only sign of age was the dry, brittle condition of the non-metal surfaces. The tires were flat. It looked like a scene in a snow globe, without the snow.

Alex said, 'I was camping alone for a couple of days before coming upon the cave. I saw the three bodies sitting in the Jeep, mummified, and thought I'd traveled back in time. I've never seen anything like this. Two days later, I walked into your office.'

Looking around, I asked Alex, 'Did you touch or disturb any-thing inside the cave?'

'No, Sheriff Cobb.'

A thought occurred to me. 'Perry, shine the flashlight on the back of their heads.'

With the help of the light, I was able to see that each body had an entrance wound located at the back of the head, with no exit. Small caliber rounds had been used to kill these three men.

'This definitely was a murder, Alex.'

'Nothing about this cave looked right, Sheriff.'

'Alex, you did the right thing, now it will be up to the coro-ner, the FBI, and the Army to find out the truth about what really happened to the three men.'

We left the cave and stood in the shade of the canyon. The walls rose up past this section some forty feet. Since the sun was lower in the sky, I estimated the time was pushing past four in the afternoon. We were able to hear the helicopter come over the canyon's ridge and land up on the mesa.

Dust and sand rained down on us from the downdraft cre-ated by the helicopter. We worked our way out of the canyon to where the horses were tethered. The men who had just landed would take fifteen minutes to get down to us. Anyone on horse-back was still two hours away.

The bodies' location presented an unexpected question beyond who killed the soldiers – why put them in this remote cave?

The FBI and the Army landed. The bodies would be flown out aboard the helicopter. It would take a week to move the Jeep from the cave and get it transported back to the lab in Independence.

The work of finding out the identities of the murdered men and when it occurred would take some time. The why, and who was responsible, would take much longer.

Chapter 7

The day after the discovery, the FBI assigned Special Agent Carl Magnus, and the U.S. Army sent CID—the Criminal Investigation Command—agent Captain Sam Ludo, and a pathologist, to perform the autopsies. During the following three weeks, the investigators found out the names of the deceased by examining the dogtags the soldiers wore, and Army records from before the war.

A picture of the entire company was found, all thirty enlised men, including First Sargeant Arnold and Major Hayes. The picture was yellow from age, but the faces of all the men were identifiable with the names of each individual written beow.

The dead soldiers in the Jeep were Private Marshall Cox, age twenty-one, of Bakersfield in Kern County; Private Harry Crenshaw, age eighteen, of Hanford in Kings County; and Private William Taylor, age nineteen, of Barstow in San Bernardino County. Their surviving families still resided in each location.

Military service records of each man related assignment to the 275th Headquarters Company of the California National Guard stationed at Fort Irwin, California, from 1938 to March 1942, were forwarded.

The 275th Headquarters Company of the California National Guard in 1942 was assigned to the 4th Infantry Division of the Oklahoma National Guard—the first National Guard unit activated in World War II in 1941. The division embarked for the Mediterranean on June 8, 1943, and landed in North Africa on June 22, 1943.

The commanding officer of Headquarters Company was Major Jamison Hayes, now retired and living in Indian Wells, in the Coachella Valley, on his father's date ranch since December 1944.

All the surviving relatives of the dead soldiers told the two investigators that the last letters they had received were dated

January 1942. The families received no further word until the War Department sent two Officers to notify each family in person, with news of the young mens' deaths. Private Marshall Cox died on September 10, 1943; Private Harry Crenshaw killed on January 23, 1944; and Private William Taylor died on February 12, 1944. A corporal, Scott Huddelson, age twenty-two, was also listed as dying in the war; his sister and only relative surviving, living in China Lake, California, had received notice of her brother's death in 1944.

The discrepancy in death notification was age, which indicated that they had all died together, sometime between January and March of 1942. Determination was done by piecing together the surrounding forensics, including the manufacturing of the Jeep, clothing on the diseased, and approximate time for the bodies to decompose in the dry desert air.

There was also the glaring error of the total number of men in the Headquarters Company from December 1941 through 1945, when they returned to California. The 275th Headquarters Company returned to the United States in May of 1945. The Company was deactivated at the California National Guard at Fort Irwin. The remaining staff was reassigned to other clerical positions or mustered out of the Army.

These three men and Corporal Scott Huddelson were the four casualties of the 275th Headquarters Company during the war. Major Hayes was injured on August 16, 1944, the result of an ambush of his vehicle northeast of Paris. He and his aide, First Seargent Wade Arnold, along with the driver, were going to 4th Division Headquarters. The French driver was killed, Major Hayes's left arm was traumatically amputated between the shoulder and elbow in the crash, and First Sergeant Arnold fought off the enemy and saved Major Hayes's life.

The company was part of the liberation forces which marched into Paris on August 24. Major Hayes was recovering in the hospital until September 1, 1944. Major Hayes was treated at two separate hospitals in France before being sent to London for further medical care.

General Lucian Hayes received news of his son's injuries and was able to get First Sergeant Arnold to accompany Jamison to London and then on the return to Southern California for further recuperation. In all physical therapy lasted in London and continued at Hayes Date Ranch in Indian Wells.

The four men of the 275th killed during the war each had a cemetery plot in the theater of war where they supposedly died. The Army sent investigators to each location to exhume the bodies and to find out who had been interred there.

The Army, Department of Defense, and the U.S. government all worked at a snail's pace when it came to investigating any abnormality in procedures. Chasing down who was responsible for the burials, death certificates, and notifications to each family meant gaining access to the unit's archives, still in storage at Ft. Irwin. The search resulted in finding everything except information about the four dead service personnel. The file was empty, as were the four graves in Europe. Where was Corporal Scott Huddelson?

Chapter 8

The Huddelson clan grew up near China Lake, a large military installation for the Navy in the Western Mojave Desert region of California, approximately 150 miles north of Los Angeles. The facility land is in three counties—Kern, San Bernardino, and Inyo. The installation's closest neighbors are the city of Ridgecrest and the communities of Inyokern, Trona, and Darwin.

China Lake is the United States Navy's largest single landholding, representing 85 percent of the Navy's land for weapons and armaments research, development, and acquisition. In total, its two ranges, and central sites cover more than 1,100,000 acres, an area larger than the state of Rhode Island.

The Huddelson family included Patrice, the oldest, her brother Scott, and three other brothers, twins named Allan and William, and Charles. In 1942, Patrice was 26, Allan and William both 24, Scott was 22, and Charles was 12.

Patrice and her family lived in an old Victorian house and had a little cattle ranch. It was off the actual Naval Base, nearer to Ridgecrest, on an unincorporated piece of land, some 200 acres. Life for the Huddelson family was hard, working all day at the ranch or in school.

Scott received more bullying than the others, with two brothers and a sister all older than him. By the time Charles came along, he was the miracle baby, and everyone left him alone. Scott was bullied at home and school. His reading was inadequate due to his dyslexia. He kept rearranging letters in words making learning more difficult. Everything changed when Scott became a teenager. He grew taller than his older siblings, and they had other things on their minds—girls for the twins and boys for Patrice.

Scott barely graduated from high school, and within a month, he joined the California National Guard in Fort Irwin. The 275th

Headquarters Company was established the year before but didn't become operational until the beginning of 1938.

The Huddelson family would send cookies to Scott and his army friends. His sergeant, Wade Arnold, made Scott write and thank his family for the gifts.

The work in the Company was routine, physical training each morning from six to seven, then breakfast, the rest of the morning doing paperwork in the office, afternoons either shooting on the rifle range or resting time in the barracks. It was a job, not fighting a war that no one ever thought was going to come to their little slice of the world. The Company had twenty-five enlisted soldiers working in shifts in the office, training exercises, or on the shooting range. They were never interacting with any other groups or personnel at the Fort.

The news of the Japanese surprise attack on Pearl Harbor took everyone in the company by surprise. They were finishing lunch when the first alert came over the loudspeaker. Their commanding officers instructed all the soldiers at Fort Irwin that war was most likely imminent with news from Europe and Asia.

I went to the door to leave, Patrice asked me to wait as she looked through a cabinet drawer finding a picture.

'Sheriff, this is a picture of Scott with all the other men from the 275th Headquarters Company of the California National Guard stationed at Fort Irwin before leaving for overseas.'

I saw all the enlisted men with First Sgt. Wade Arnold and Major Hayes. Scot was in the second row. The names of the soldiers were captioned at the bottom of the picture.

'Thank you, Patrice.' I put the picture in glove compartment.

Chapter 9

Owen Snyder called just as I put my hand on my office door to leave for Indian Wells to interview retired Major Jamison Hayes and First Sergeant Wade Arnold.

Owen said, 'I received a letter from my brother Wally. The letter details what he saw in January 1942. He wanted me to give the information to you.'

'I'm on my way out to Indian Wells, but I'll stop by on the way.'

I gathered my hat and walked past Marlene Chambers' dispatch desk. She looked up and said, 'Sheriff, Alex Morgan came in to ask about the bodies found at Malpais Mesa.'

'I don't see him here, Marlene.'

'He was here just a minute ago; Edith was talking with him. Maybe they went to the breakroom.'

I walked into the breakroom as Edith handed Alex Morgan a steaming cup of coffee. 'Alex, did you want to see me?'

'Yes, Sheriff, any news about the bodies I found?' Alex asked as Edith poured herself a cup.

I'd expected he would want to know. 'A press conference is scheduled for tomorrow at the FBI Office in Los Angeles.'

Alex nodded. 'Is there any news, off the record, for a local rancher?'

'Sure. All three men were in the Army. The FBI and Army CID located the surviving families.' I paused a moment, glancing at Edith. 'I'm on my way out to interview the man who was their commanding officer when they were stationed at Fort Irwin.'

Alex groaned. 'I guess the rest of the information will be told at the news conference.'

'Yes, Alex, but I doubt the information presented will answer any question you may have. It seems that the mystery deepens with each revelation.'

I noticed Edith standing next to Alex, and the look in her eyes reminded me of watching a cougar on a granite ledge, ready to pounce on its prey.

Edith has always been good at getting all the facts she needs about people who came into the sheriff's office. Alex Morgan was a widower with two adult sons who worked with him on his ranch. Neither son was married. Alex hadn't dated since the loss of his wife to breast cancer six years ago. Was Edith looking to find a place at the Morgan ranch?

I'd previously seen Edith get tangled up with Barton Haskel and then Grady Bennett. Each relationship ended with Edith not hooking her lasso onto a shining star, but on something that was only temporary and, in the end, hurtful. However, she was the most resilient human being I've ever known. She would find her happy place, and we in the sheriff's department would celebrate with her.

I tipped my hat at the lean, rangy cowboy as he and Edith talked with each other. I needed to hustle to read the letter from Wally Snyder and make the drive down to Indian Wells. The way my day was going, anything could turn up.

Chapter 10

Alex Morgan accepted the coffee from Edith. 'Black, concentrated, and powerful enough to get through the day, just like I like it.'

Edith's face lit up like a Fourth of July fireworks display. 'I called your home a few days ago, and your son Craig told me how you liked your coffee.'

Edith kept the conversation professional. She didn't want anyone in the department knowing that she and Alex were getting together at her bungalow, since the day after he walked into the sheriff's office with his discovery of three bodies in a cave near Malpais Mesa.

Alex looked at Edith with more than thanks for the coffee.

'There is no official statement at this time, Mr. Morgan. Sheriff Cobb said that the FBI, along with the Army, and our department will hold a press conference in LA tomorrow; however, the news Jim just let slip is all new to me, I guess we will all have to wait for more information.'

Edith rolled her hands together, fumbling as she said, 'Is there…anything else…Mr. Morgan?' Moisture started to form on her upper lip in anticipation of what Alex would say next.

'No, Miss Pearson, nothing else today. I'll just go over to the Morning Cup Coffee Shop, have breakfast, and read today's paper, thank you.' He disposed of his empty cardboard coffee cup in the wastebasket and left.

Edith knew the lie, and the subterfuge was for Marlene's benefit. The code left no misunderstanding as to the location of his next stop.

Marlene snorted at Edith, 'Looks like Mr. Morgan wants to have breakfast and more coffee. If you're not interested, I'll take my break now and keep him company.'

'No, Marlene, I'll enjoy my break now,' Edith retorted and left the office with her purse in hand. She wasn't going to let this fish off her hook, and she wasn't going to allow the office gossip to swipe her catch.

Edith and Marlene had had a cantankerous, marginal relationship since Edith had come on board as the secretary for Merrill Cobb, years ago. Edith saw all of Marlene's gyrations to get Merrill into her bed, but the old man became very nervous whenever the subject was broached. Edith was having fun with Barton Haskel until Lara Aartz came into the picture. Edith and Marlene each knew about what they wanted from the men in their lives, happiness, and safety, but Marlene had become vindictive over the years when her wishes were not met.

Marlene had told false stories to Barton about other men to break them up, Edith and Barton. She had even called up Grady Bennett, the reporter from the *LA Post*, to scare him into not writing stories about the Hanging Murderer and the murder of Barton Haskel. Marlene had tried to cover for Merrill's lack of success in capturing the Hanging Murderer, who turned out to be Silas Reid.

Edith arrived at the coffee shop, walking toward Alex. He surrounded her as he pulled her close to his chest and covered her mouth with his. The couple broke apart; Edith was a little unsteady on her feet after Alex's onslaught. She told him, 'Marlene is tenacious about finding out where I'm going and who I'm with.'

'Marlene is an old crone living in the past, where she may have been at the top of the heap. Now she is just a lonely person with only her dreams of another time.' Alex replied.

'Keeping her at bay makes my whole day. Shall we proceed, Mr. Morgan?'

Chapter 11

I arrived at the Lone Pine Pharmacy to see Owen. The stocky pharmacist, his leg brace creaking, stepped out from behind the high counter and motioned me to follow him through the door to his small office behind the prescription preparation area.

Owen moved behind his little desk, produced an envelope, and handed it to me as I sat in the visitor's chair. I read the letter inside, then replaced it.

'Owen, when did you receive this?'

'With today's morning mail.'

Looking at him, I asked, 'What is your take on the information Wally wrote?'

'Sheriff, my brother is an honest man. He has no reason to lie. I believe what he has written.'

'He doesn't say anything about his whereabouts.' I checked the front of the envelope. 'I see it's postmarked from Los Angeles...any idea if he's still there?'

'No, Jim. This letter is the only thing I've received. I'm pretty worried.'

'Owen, I'm headed down to Indian Wells to interview a couple of men about the three bodies found out at Malpais Mesa. I'll give this letter to Red Fowler and have him take a few people out to this location near Furnace Creek to see what he can find. I'll also have someone go out to his trailer. In the meantime, I don't want you to say anything to anyone about the contents of this letter, including your wife.'

Owen developed a definite sheen of perspiration on his forehead. He gulped, then said, 'I've never kept anything from Emily since the first day I met her in grade school.'

'Okay, Owen, tell Emily in private and impress upon her that I don't want either one of you to utter a word about the information Wally wrote in this letter.'

Owen let out a sigh of relief. 'Okay, Jim, Emily, and I will not tell a soul.'

'I'm going to ask again; do you have any idea where Wally is or who he may be with?'

'No, Jim, Wally didn't tell me or anyone in my family what he was doing before he left. I never even knew anyone he associated with Inyo County.'

I thought a moment. 'Any war buddies from his time in the Army?'

Shaking his head, Owen replied, 'Wally talked about GIs he met, but none lived on the West Coast.'

'Thanks, Owen, if you or Emily can think of anyone, give my office a call.'

I left the pharmacy and changed my plan for the day—instead of going on to Indian Wells, I headed back to the office.

The information Wally wrote in his letter to his brother was troublesome. If it was true, then my little corner of the world was going to splash big on the national scene. This news wasn't going to sit well with any veteran who fought in the Pacific, let alone anyone in Southern California.

Chapter 12

I returned to the office and relayed the information in the letter to Red Fowler. Red was aghast at the particulars but agreed to visit Death Valley with a couple of men to seek out the location described in the letter. If anything was found, I instructed Red to make the area a crime scene and bring out the necessary equipment and personnel.

I wrote in a private file the information contained in the letter from Wally to Owen. I knew keeping a record of everything about this case was going to be vital.

I made sure Red knew where I was going, then I headed to Indian Wells. According to a brochure printed by the Chamber of Commerce, the first Desert Classic Golf Tournament had been won by Arnold Palmer two years ago, in 1960, and President Dwight D. Eisenhower was a regular visitor to the Indian Wells area.

The vast desert of California's Coachella Valley, which stretches from Palm Springs to the Salton Sea, represents the center of the nation's date palm industry, and the Hayes Ranch was started by General Lucian Richmond Hayes, father of Jamison Hayes, in the 1890s.

The afternoon was bright and warm, without a cloud in the cobalt blue sky.

I arrived at the Hayes date ranch in Indian Wells to interview retired Major Jamison Hayes and retired First Sergeant Wade Arnold.

The front door was answered by a Chinese housemaid, her facial features drawn, dressed in a dull gray uniform. Her accent was formal British, indicating an education. The woman wasn't much over five feet and no more than ninety pounds soaking wet. She stood ramrod straight, as if she had a military background.

The housemaid told me that Major Hayes was out of the country, but Wade Arnold, the ranch's overseer, would meet me in the solarium. The imposing glassed area was fifty square feet in size, with ornate furniture from the Victorian Age and a substantial array of exotic plants. The plants ranged from palms to orchids in a sea of high humidity, something the fortunate desert dwellers in the area never experienced.

Due to all the sunlight, the room was cooled by a refrigeration system that delivered cold air from several different grated inserts in the wooden floors. Without the AC, the room would have been unbearable.

Wade Arnold was seated in the center of the room in a leather wingback chair. Arnold had thinning, dark brown hair and the most piercing black eyes I'd ever seen. He sat straight and tall, not a hint of any muscle weaknesses, and looked like a bird of prey ready to swoop down and capture its next meal.

'Mr. Arnold, I presume,' I said as he stood. He was almost six feet tall. We shook hands firmly. His tan face and arms, thick hands and barrel chest resonated hard work in the sun. His appearance showed he took care of all things around the date farm.

Wade Arnold stared through me as he said, 'Glad to meet you, Sheriff Cobb; what can we do for you?'

I noted that he had said 'we' but I didn't comment on that. 'We found three of your missing soldiers, dead, sitting in one of your Headquarters Company's Jeeps in a cave below Malpais Mesa, near Death Valley.'

I took a breath, watching his face as I spoke. 'The mummified remains of Private Marshall Cox, age twenty-one; Private Harry Crenshaw, age eighteen; and Private William Taylor, age nineteen.'

'Yes, we here at the ranch know all about your findings,' he said.

Mr. Arnold's nonchalant attitude was unsettling to me. I must have given my feelings away because he said, 'Don't be taken aback, Sheriff. We were informed of your discovery and the subsequent inquiry from the FBI and Army CID last week. We are very well-informed, thanks to the nature of Major Hayes's position with the Army and the local community.'

'It is certainly good luck that Major Hayes and you are so well-informed,' I replied.

'Yes, it is Sheriff Cobb. The Coachella Valley has a long history of helping prominent families, especially if they are revered in the military. Anything else?' Arnold asked, his eyes never flickering.

'Yes,' I said, wondering if I would get any useful information from him. 'The three soldiers we found in the cave, how did they get there, and when?'

'Let me tell you the sad story, Sheriff. Three young men were from families known to General Lucian Richmond Hayes. The parents reached out to the general in 1940 and asked if their sons could be part of the unit Major Hayes was assembling at Fort Irwin after they enlisted in the Army. They all came to the 275th. Unfortunately, these three didn't have the guts to fight the enemy after the sudden attack by the Japanese. They deserted several days after December 7. They hightailed it out of Fort Irwin and across the border into Mexico. Unfortunately, they ran into some unsavory individuals down there and were killed. Three of my men and I found their shallow graves and brought them home.'

Questions popped into my head.

How did they know about these unsavory individuals? How did they know where the graves were? And finally, why bring the bodies back at all? The story made no sense.

Smelling the lies, I interrupted to ask, 'When did this happen?'

'It was December 20, 1941. Corporal Scott Huddelson was one of the soldiers who accompanied me into Mexico. After retrieval of the bodies, Major Hayes insisted we keep the families uninformed about what the boys had done. The Corporal, who was from the China Lake area in Kern County, knew about the hidden cave and suggested the interment site.' Arnold paused a moment before continuing. 'The families were told their loved ones died in battle.'

Curious to see how he would answer, I asked just one thing. 'Why?'

Arnold shrugged. 'Sheriff, the major, and I felt it was kinder to the families. No family wanted to be associated with the black mark of desertion, which these three men performed. It was, let us say, a command decision on the major's part. No harm, no foul.'

As I finished writing, I told him, 'The news of your actions will come out now, Mr. Arnold.'

Arnold nodded. 'Yes, I'm sure it will. The major informed the families this morning before he left on a trip outside the country. Even though the soldiers deserted their post, Major Hayes has a strong devotion to all the men who served under him in the war.'

'You said the Major left this morning?' I said, looking around the room. 'Where did he go?'

With a slight smile, he replied, 'The family has a large hacienda, with landholdings and a coffee plantation in Costa Rica. The trip was planned several months ago and is a routine sojourn twice a year. Major Hayes will be there for the next couple of months. Is there anything else, Sheriff?'

'Yeah, there is.' I had a few more questions, even if he wanted me gone, 'Where is Corporal Huddelson?'

Arnold turned to look at the orchid next to him. 'I was informed through military channels that the corporal died as a real hero, when the company crossed the Siegfried Line, on March 17, 1945. A tragic loss, but a more endearing lost to the Major. Major Hayes loved Corporal Huddelson like a son. The Major and I returned to Coachella Valley just before Christmas, December 1944, needing more recovery from his war injury. We were informed of the Corporal's death by Headquarters Company.'

I asked, 'Did your unit suffer any casualties other than Corporal Huddelson and the three dead soldiers found near Malpais Mesa?'

Mr. Arnold shook his head. 'No, Sheriff, Headquarters Company was behind the lines in secure quarters.'

'Okay… but wait.' I paused a moment to think. 'When Major Hayes was injured, wasn't the driver killed?'

'Yes, he was, but that soldier—oh, I don't recall his name—was from the 4th Infantry Division, only assigned to drive the Major around, but not attached to Headquarters Company. Anything else I can help you with, Sheriff?' Mr. Arnold offered a Cheshire Cat's grin.

The ride back to Independence was long and uneventful, giving me time to think about what Wade Arnold said, including Major Hayes leaving the country and the death of Corporal Scott Huddelson. No one was left to contradict his statements. The retired First Sergeant knew how to give a pittance of information and hide the rest, without making it look like an out and out lie. Every question had an answer—all nice and tidy.

The information getting to Indian Wells last week? From whom? The deaths of three servicemen, who had presumably deserted? Finding the bodies in Mexico? How did Arnold know they met unsavory individuals, and why bring back the bodies and put them in a cave?

I placed the entire conversation in the category of a cover-up.

I'd get Edith to investigate the hacienda in Costa Rica, any more information about the date ranch in Indian Wells, and any other property the Hayes Family owns.

I put aside the information from Indian Wells and wondered what, if anything, Red had found in Death Valley.

Chapter 13

January of 1910 brought a massive snowstorm to the High Sierras in California. The eastern slope didn't receive as much, but it was more than enough for the Arnold family on their little cattle ranch south of Owens Lake in Inyo County.

The Arnold ranch was a rundown scrap of land with never any more than twenty head of cattle, not enough to make a decent living, but just enough money for whiskey to keep Henry Arnold drunk six days out of seven.

Fortune had not come to the Arnold household. Infant mortality was high, 100 per 1,000 births. Three children lost before the age of four, one to pertussis (whooping cough), another to measles, and the third to diphtheria – there were no vaccines for these diseases. This time, the outcome would be different.

Kara, his mother named the new baby after a teacher she'd had in school in Nebraska. The boy's name was Wade. This boy was big at birth, over nine pounds, much bigger than the first three, but neither the mother nor father knew that the large size presented a harbinger of danger for the mother. Her affliction was from this second type of diabetes, *sugar*, its name at the time. This disease doesn't let the patient make insulin (a peptide hormone produced by beta cells of the pancreas).

Diabetes is a terrible disease, sneaky, insidious, as it traverses someone's body until finally, they form black discolorations on a toe without any pain. In time the appendage becomes entirely black and dead, falling off without the individual even knowing it. Walking may not be affected at first unless it was the big toe, but there is no stopping the progression. Non-traumatic amputations frequently occurred without the individual, even realizing it.

Some might say like Sherman's march to the sea, no amount of 'Johnny Rebs' could reverse the onslaught.

In 1917, there was no money for a doctor, and there wasn't much a doctor could do. Sugar was a disease that ravaged an innocent patient. The symptoms of excessive thirst, urination, and hunger devastated the individuals, making them overweight. Kara, survived for several more years, even though the food was sparse, and her husband beat her whenever he was drunk.

Kara kept falling. She had little or no feeling in her lower legs; the disease affected her nerves, reducing any pain. She'd already lost two toes on one foot and three on the other. One night, after drinking more than usual, Henry hit her with several backhanded blows to her face and a punch to her stomach. This time she didn't get up.

The next morning Wade, by now six or seven, saw his mother on the floor in the kitchen, not moving. The boy didn't know what to do, but one thing he did know; not to say anything to his daddy. Before his father came in, he went and huddled in his bed, crying.

Henry awoke, staggered into the kitchen, saw his dead wife on the floor, and heard his son snoring in his bed. Overtaken by fear, he picked up Kara and took her out to the barn, placed her on the buckboard wagon with a shovel, and rode off. He came back alone an hour later. Henry told Wade and other people that Kara had run off to parts unknown.

Henry kept drinking, only now he took his frustration out on Wade. He used his fists, a switch, or a belt to keep the boy in line. Wade learned, through experience, to not talk back, or it would be worse. He took his beatings without saying a word. Wade had only one thing in his favor. He kept growing, bigger, and stronger, until he turned sixteen.

Henry had been drinking moonshine ever since Prohibition became the law of the land. The 'white lightning' wasn't right, but it did the trick, it made Henry drunk.

Wade was working in the barn, fixing the buckboard wagon, when Henry came out looking for a fight.

'Boy, what the fuck are you doing?'

Wade looked at his father in disgust. 'I'm fixing the wagon you broke.'

'Don't sass me, boy.' Henry couldn't stand up straight. He weaved his way to his son while pulling off his belt. He wrapped the end around his hand, raised the strap over his head with the buckle at the end, ready to strike.

Wade had a wooden ax handle next to his leg. Before Henry could lower the belt, Wade swung the ax handle like he was swinging for the fences in a baseball game. The blow hit Henry on his left upper abdomen, breaking some ribs, and forcing his father to double over, clutching his midriff. Vomiting, he fell on the dirt floor of the barn.

Writhing in pain, he yelled out, 'Boy, you better run, because if I catch you, I'll kill you, like I did your mother!'

His face contorted with rage, Wade swung the wooden club down on his father's head, 'No, you old drunk, you're not hurting anyone else ever again!'

Henry's nose was broken, and blood was pouring from his face into the dirt.

Wade looked at his father's motionless body, waiting for the sorrow, the regret to overtake him. It never came. He felt nothing. Leaving the barn, he went into the house and gathered up what belonged to him. He found some money his father had hidden, walked out to the highway, and stuck out his thumb. Soon, a truck came by and drove him to San Bernardino.

Wade exited the vehicle and thanked the driver for the ride. He looked around and walked into the nearest store, a pharmacy. On the wall was a pay telephone. He didn't have much money, but he got some change from the man who worked the soda fountain and called the Sheriff's Office in Inyo County. He told the woman in the Sheriff's office that he was a truck driver who picked up a young kid, who said he was sixteen and lived at the Arnold ranch. The kid said that his father fell from the loft in the barn, and the dad looked hurt bad. The truck driver said he was calling from Bakersfield.

Wade hung up before the woman asked any questions. He let them assume the kid left the ranch, not knowing what to do.

Working on some ranches in San Bernardino was okay in the spring of 1926. Wade figured he could do it for a few months. He didn't know what had happened when the sheriff went out to the ranch to check on Henry in the barn.

Wade decided to head for the Coachella Valley. He'd heard the weather was better there, plus there were many farms and ranches where he could find work. One guy he worked with mentioned the Hayes' Date Palm Ranch

Wade found the Hayes' ranch in mid-June and Ballard and Florence Hayes took a liking to the silent, hard-working kid. He never left.

In September, Wade asked, 'Mrs. Hayes, is there any place where I might be able to read newspapers from other parts of the state?'

'Yes, Wade, the library in Palm Springs has several papers from around the state and the major cities in the country. I can take you there on Saturday.'

'That's swell, Mrs. Hayes, but I don't want to put you out any.'

'It's my pleasure. Saturday it is, we can go around eleven.'

Wade smiled at his kind boss and went back to work.

Saturday, eleven a.m., found Wade standing next to the car Mrs. Hayes would drive.

'All set to go?' Florence Hayes asked Wade as she came out of the kitchen door of her house and walked to her car.

'Yes, Ma'am, all set.' Wade opened the passenger door and sat in the car for the ride to the library in Palm Springs.

Florence and Wade went into the library together. Florence introduced Wade to the librarian. The librarian was an older woman around sixty, her brown and gray hair in a bun at the back of her head.

Wade said, 'I'm interested in newspapers from Inyo County.'

'Yes, we have the paper from Lone Pine,' the librarian replied.

Wade nodded.

The librarian brought the young man to the reading room in the back of the library, were newspapers from the *Lone Pine Centennial* were stored. Wade said, 'I'm interested in the papers after April 15 of this year.'

The librarian smiled. 'The newest copy is on top of this stack, and it should go back to the first of the year. The *Centennial* is a twice-weekly paper.'

'Yes, I know, thank you for all your help.'

Wade found the papers for April, quickly searched the headlines and the obituaries. None of the newspapers mentioned the accident. He did find an issue from the end of May, in the obituaries. 'Henry Arnold passed away today after suffering a tragic fall from the loft of his barn on April 19. A call came into the Inyo Sheriff's Department on the morning of April 20, stating a truck driver called to inform the Sheriff about a fall Mr. Arnold sustained in the barn by himself. Mr. Arnold suffered from a broken nose and jaw, also internal injuries to his spleen and a loss of blood. Surgery saved his life for three weeks, but an infection developed, causing his death. Mr. Arnold's only relative, his sixteen-yer-old son, Wade, is no longer living in Inyo County.'

Wade read the article three times to understand the implication. He killed his father like his father killed his mother. No tears shed for the man who bore him. Wade had no intention of ever returning to the Owens Lake area or seeing the old homestead. There was nothing there left for him. The county buried his worthless father, and he had no idea about his mother's burial site. Wade replaced the newspapers in an orderly fashion as he found them. He walked to the front of the library and found Florence.

Florence asked Wade, 'Did you find what you were looking for?'

Wade nodded. 'Yes, the news I was interested in telling me about a new addition to the one-room high school I went to in Owens Valley.

Wade couldn't understand how he could lie so comfortably to Mrs. Hayes, regarding his father's death—just a small ripple in a pond of scum.

Chapter 14

The scruffy man in the faded dark blue truck stopped in Thermal, California, a town of approximately twelve-hundred people, mostly Mexican. He ate at a taco stand, like many day laborers in the community did, and found out from short conversations that the place to go at night was *El Caminante,* The Wayfarer Bar. The beer was cold and the *chicas* were hot.

Just before two in the morning, closing time, the man saw two women, one a little older, a little heavier, the other a diminutive girl who looked about seventeen or eighteen, no more than five-foot-two, with big brown eyes and breasts to match. He caught her eye, but she played hard to get at the beginning. The dance began in the sweltering night heat of Thermal.

Over Coronas, he learned her friend's name was Lupe, hers was Margarita, and she was from Tecate, a small city in Baja California, Mexico, some forty miles south of San Diego. Her parents had ridden the wave of illegal Mexican immigrants to California. They had sought wealth and riches, but found only farm labor, until they died in a car accident. Little eleven-year-old Margarita survived the accident.

She was sent to Sisters of Perpetual Mercy Orphanage by her two older brothers, Luis, age seventeen and Jose, age fifteen. Luis told the orphanage their parents and an older brother died in a car crash. Jose said the Margarita was fourteen when she was only eleven. Neither brother could take care of themselves, let alone a sister.

El Caminante was closed.

Margarita, smiling to make some money this night, pushed open the door to her room at the back of the bar with her hip, turned on the bare bulb, the room sparse but clean, the bed big enough for two.

Margarita faced him, unbuttoned her blouse, and threw it in the corner. His eyes widened at the sight of her, wanting to grab the encased orbs in each hand. He licked his lips in anticipation.

Margarita said, 'Yes, big boy, they are real, and they are all yours for the night, plus much more, for five dollars.'

The man smiled and removed the sawbuck from his pants pocket, laying it on her battered dresser.

Margarita unhooked her bra and slipped it off.

The man flipped off the light switch and put his hands around her waist, drawing her closer to him as he covered her mouth with his. She locked her arms behind his neck. Neither could get enough of the other.

'For a scruffy *gringo*, you know how to warm a woman up.'

'This is just the beginning, *chica*.'

Neither had ever experienced this level of sexual satisfaction from another human being.

After a shower in the communal bath down the hall from Margarita's room, they drove to a diner for breakfast. They returned satiated from the meal, but not from each other. Closing the door to her room, they enjoyed each other until sunset came on the farming community. A knock from the bartender awoke Margarita, his voice demanding that she wait tables in the bar.

The couple looked at each other and without saying a word, dressed in silence, packed a cardboard suitcase with all of Margarita's earthly belongings, and surreptitiously retreated out the back door.

The couple rode in the truck until they found an out-of-the-way motel and started again. Neither talked for fear that the magical experience they each were living might just end without warning. The man had lost the urge to kill. Margarita, at last, had her man.

After they had satiated each other, Margarita rolled over and ran her fingers along his jawline.

'Well, after all that…what shall I call you?' Margarita asked.

He had never told anyone his real name. Looking at Margarita in the dim light, he felt close to her, safe with her. Content for the first time, he smiled as he answered, 'Just call me JB.'

After revealing his name, he thought about where he came from. He remembered his mother, in one of her few softer moments, telling him how it all started... back in 1920 along the Columbia River in Washington State.

His parents were Linwood and Juanita Todd, and they met in El Paso, on a cold and blustery night. Juanita had swum across the Rio Grande and landed in the campsite Linwood had set up a week earlier. He was originally from Kent, England but had immigrated a year earlier on a tramp steamer, after deserting from the English Army in the Great War. The auspicious meeting was in January 1916.

They had traveled and camped outdoors together through-out the southwest, into California and north to Washington. JB's birth had been in March of 1920. The inauspicious beginning was a harbinger of a hard life. When JB was ten, his mother gave him away to some migrant family headed south to pick vegeta-bles in the Salinas Valley.

He worked and traveled with the Mexican family of laborers for six seasons, watching and learning from others in the migrant camps. This is how he learned to use a knife to defend oneself and to be a predator. The father, or *el jefe*, would slap and hit him in the head almost every day—for not working fast or hard enough, and even for overeating.

One day in late August, when it was hot, and the stoop labor was hard, *el jefe* started a fight with another boy in the family, a year younger than JB. The assault was brutal, the boy's nose was broken, and blood covered his face. JB took out his folding knife before he realized what he was going to do and held the six-inch blade with both hands above his head. He felt a bolt of lightning run through him as he rammed the point into *el jefe's* back, puncturing his lung. The older man fell to his knees and turned white as his chest filled with blood.

No one in the camp said a word as they watched the death of *el jefe*. Another man grabbed JB by his shirt and told him to run, run far away. *El jefe* had many relatives working in the camps, and if anyone found out what he had done, JB would be marked for death.

JB stole the 1928 Model A truck owned by *el jefe* and headed to Bakersfield. He didn't know anyone in Bakersfield, he just wanted to get as far away as he could before the cops showed up. Under the front seat, he found a pistol wrapped in an old oil-covered cloth.

JB ran into one of the migrant workers from Salinas, after the war, and found out the police were never called. It seemed everyone hated *el jefe,* and they were thankful he'd set them free from the tyrant. The truck had been stolen from a ranch before he'd joined the family, and everyone was glad when he drove off with it.

Thinking about his first kill, JB would remember it as luck, pure and simple. But that feeling of control, of having someone else's life in your hands, was pure ecstasy, and he wanted to catch that lightning in a bottle again and again. JB had killed a hated man, someone the family was glad to be rid of. He took a truck no one wanted around, and with it, he had a chance to find a life without anyone telling him what to do.

JB didn't worry about the draft when it came at the start of the war, He never paid taxes, filled out a census bureau card, or signed up for the draft. JB was a no one, no person, no identity, a nameless, faceless, person in the great outdoors.

He was free from a lifetime of beatings by men he wasn't related to, poverty, drunkenness, and watching the abuse of women and children. He settled on a new name and an outlook that catered only to him—selfish, self-centered, and egotistical, his mistreatment of women and children, and of wanting to control or kill those weaker than he was. That is until he found Margarita.

Some call its kismet; others might say fate when two people enter each other's orbit and understand instantly that they are inevitability linked together without words or station in life. These two had something they didn't understand or comprehend. Something that, if they could bottle the sensation, would make them more prosperous than they imagined.

The future...unknown at the start of the journey, but who cares when you are having fun, just enjoy the ride. That was their motto. Enjoy the ride the two did, daily, nightly, anytime, without reason, just a look from either, and the other responded.

Chapter 15

I arrived home after my long drive to Indian Wells around eight o'clock in the evening. Conchita had prepared *posole*, a Mexican soup made with whole hominy, my absolute favorite. I had finished two bowls of soup when Conchita sat down next to me at the kitchen table.

She said, 'Jim, did the long drive to Indian Wells answer any questions?'

'No, the man I talked with, Wade Arnold, told me a story that made no sense and only caused me to think of more questions.'

'The children are all in bed, asleep.' Conchita smiled as she continued, 'Take a hot bath, and after, I will massage your tired muscles, so you can have a restful sleep tonight.'

Making love to my wife was more vigorous than usual. We clawed at each other as if we hadn't seen each other in months. Conchita knew all the buttons to push on my tired body, allowing me to satisfy her in more ways than I had since the three dead soldiers were found.

Conchita rolled off my chest with a sheen of sweat on her body. She enjoyed making love until we could no longer move, talk, or think. Her head lay on my chest, safe, secure, and satisfied as we each drifted off into the most restful sleep imaginable.

I awoke the next morning to the sound of our three children enjoying breakfast at the kitchen table.

I cleaned up and dressed, walked into the kitchen, kissed Conchita good morning, and kissed each boy as I rubbed their heads before settling in front of Rosie's highchair. The little charmer knew she had me wrapped around her little finger, just like her mother. She sat with her chin in her hands, her elbows on the tray of her highchair, looking directly into my eyes.

Rosie said in her soft voice, 'Good sleep, Daddy?'

'My little Princess Cupcake.'

Rosie smiled and laughed at me.

Conchita made me *huevos rancheros*, with Monterey Jack cheese, cilantro, *salsa*, and black beans. I was in heaven, having a great meal with my wife and children around me.

Taking a bite of food, Conchita said, 'Jim, I forgot to tell you last night, but Delfina and Merrill are coming next week.'

'Fantastic, I can't wait to see the old codger. How long will they be staying?' I asked.

Delfina's background, family history, and whereabouts before meeting Merrill were all cloaked in secrecy. Merrill had taken me aside and told me not to ask, as it didn't matter to him and was no concern for me.

I wasn't interested in Delfina's past, if she kept Merrill happy, satisfied, and in Zihuatanejo.

Conchita jolted me out of my reverie when she said, 'Delfina was talking about staying here a couple of weeks. They also want to drive around Southern California and Arizona.'

I shrugged. 'I guess the old codger is happy with his living arrangement in Mexico.'

'I think that they both are happy,' Conchita answered.

Tickling Rosie, I asked, 'When do they plan to arrive?'

Pouring orange juice for the boys, Conchita replied, 'They land next week in Los Angeles. A little looking around there, and then drive up here, maybe three days later.'

'Whatever makes them happy. I will be too busy to entertain my father and the love of his life.' I paused and looked at her 'I hope you don't mind entertaining them in my absence?'

Conchita smiled at me. 'No, *mi hermana*, Rosita will be their guide.' Rosita, her husband and their six children were my wife's only living relatives.

Thinking that Conchita's sister, was going to act as a guide made me even more curious as to what the visitors were up to. At present, I didn't want any more information, I needed to get to work. Keeping the peace at home was what Conchita felt was her responsibility.

I knew my father and his paramour would enjoy their trip, seeing the grandkids, old friends, and relaxing in familiar surroundings. I loved my dad, even though he had exasperated me growing up, working in the Sheriff's Department, and during the Barton Haskel murder investigation.

Chapter 16

I arrived at my office at eight o'clock, in the middle of what looked like utter chaos, but was organized confusion, put in place by my competent second-in-command, Red Fowler. Police officers were hurrying all over the place, not only sheriff's deputies but CID officers and FBI agents.

FBI Agent Carl Magnus and Army CID Agent Sam Ludo were both on the phones.

I caught up with Red as he was coming out of the breakroom. 'What's going on?'

Red looked tired but determined. 'Jim, I returned here after two a.m. I left the crime scene in Death Valley with FBI, CID, and our personnel in place, with portable lighting from generators, brought in from Fort Irwin.'

Confused, I said, 'Hold on a minute, Red, start from the beginning.'

'Yesterday morning, you gave me the letter Wally Snyder sent to his brother Owen. Three deputies and I went out to the site west of Furnace Creek Road, in Death Valley.' Gesturing toward the men on the phones, Red continued, 'I called Jubal Morgan to bring out a couple of his bloodhounds to find any bodies buried out there.'

'I bet Jubal smelled worse than his dogs,' I replied.

Red nodded. 'Yes, he did, Jim, but the damn dogs went to an area sixty by twenty feet long and started digging and howling to beat the band. Jubal couldn't control the dogs. I had a couple of the boys dig where the dogs were making the most noise, and about eight or nine feet down, we found a body with his hands tied behind his back. The man looked Asian. We'll have wait until the ME, Dr. Crowley, looks at the bodies, to find out all the particulars.'

After a deep breath, Red continued, 'I had Carl Swanson drive back to the office to call out the FBI, CID, and Army to come out to examine the burial site. Forensic people, the mortician, and a backhoe were brought out, along with portable lights. When I left, the crew had found eighty-six bodies, and they think there are more buried out there.'

I couldn't grasp the magnitude of what Red was telling me. I was without words to respond to the news. All I could say was, 'Red, stay on top of these developments. I'm going to talk with Magnus and Ludo.'

Carl Magnus, fifty-two-years-old and of Norwegian ancestry, whose grandfather immigrated in 1880, grew up in a small farming community outside of Minneapolis. He was six-feet-three-inches tall, with a full head of stiff gray hair, deep blue eyes, and the build of a college linebacker—Special Agent with the FBI since 1932.

Sam Ludo, a forty-eight-year-old West Point graduate, was born and grew up in Holland, Michigan, and married his high school sweetheart. Ludo made Major before retiring from active duty in 1960 and moving over to CID as an investigator. He was always smiling, with hazel eyes, square facial features, and the body of a man who visited the gym regularly. At almost six feet, he cast a silhouette of a leading man in the movies, but his down-home demeanor was relaxed and easygoing.

I went to see the two special agents as Red hurried off to keep working the burial site. Both agents were on the phone. I waited until both were finished and relayed the information I'd garnered from Wade Arnold.

Ludo said, 'The three families of the dead soldiers found near Malpais Mesa all called in, telling us the information you were told by Wade Arnold was the same they received during the war. It is getting to sound more like Wade and Hayes are behind whatever went on, before the war and since.'

Looking at the two men, I asked, 'Do either of you know who told Hayes and Arnold about the discovery?'

Ludo, from the Army CID, answered. 'News reached Ft. Irwin when we asked about the Jeep. I would guess that Hayes and Arnold still have a close tie to the Fort, and the news was relayed to Indian Wells.'

The answer made sense. No one was told to keep the news secret. Now, this unearthing of bodies in Death Valley would surely reach Hayes and Arnold.

I asked, 'What else is going on with the mass burial site in Death Valley?'

'The FBI has called in twenty people statewide to work with the L.A. County medical examiner. While the FBI has pulled more than twenty people in for the forensics, they also are sending in three forensic pathologists/anthropologists from the Smithsonian in Washington, D.C.,' Magnus reported.

Ludo added, 'The Army is looking at all the deaths of 275th Headquarters Company of the California National Guard under Major Hayes, starting from December 7, 1941, through the end of the war.'

I checked my notes. 'When did they deploy overseas?'

'The 4th Division, which the 275th Headquarters Company was assigned to in March 1942, relocated to Fort Riley, Kansas; all personnel sailed for the Mediterranean region on June 8, 1943, ready for combat. They landed in North Africa on June 22, 1943, after the Allies had largely secured the African theater. The 4th Division, with the 275th Headquarters Company, stayed in Morocco for training until the invasion of Sicily on July 10, 1943,' Ludo said.

I stated, 'The first death reported was on September 10, 1943, after the landing at Salerno; Private Marshall Cox, age twenty-one. Crenshaw, age eighteen, died on January 23, 1944, after the landing at Anzio, and Taylor on February 12, 1944, at a place known as the Pimlott Line, the perimeter of the Anzio beachhead.'

We sat thinking about the information, before I asked the two agents, 'Is there any connection between Furnace Creek Road and the 275th Headquarters Company?'

Ludo answered, 'The 275th Headquarters Company was stationed at Fort Irwin from 1938 until leaving to join up with the 4th Infantry Division in Fort Riley in March 1942. After the Anzio invasion, the 275th Headquarters Company was sent to England and placed in the 3rd Army. They were with rear echelon troops. They landed in Normandy on June 10, 1944.' Ludo continued, 'This Headquarters Company never saw any action in the war. They were always in the rear. Major Hayes had enough influence, through his father, up the chain of command, to keep his troops and himself out of the line of fire.'

Magnus asked, 'How far is Fort Irwin from here?'

'Fort Irwin is roughly forty miles northeast of Barstow, California, and Barstow a good one hundred sixty miles from Independence,' I replied.

Ludo ran a hand through his hair. 'We need to ask Wade Arnold where he and Major Hayes were from December 8, 1941, until they joined up with 4th Infantry Division in March 1942.'

I agreed and added, 'We need to find out more about how Major Hayes lost his arm under enemy fire before the liberation of Paris.'

Marlene alerted me that Red had called on the radio, stating that another forty-two bodies were uncovered out at Furnace Creek.

I was shocked. 'The recovered body count is now up to one hundred sixty-one.'

Magnus said, 'Let me and Ludo take a run at Wade Arnold and go find Major Hayes.'

Nodding, I replied, 'I hope you get more answers than I did.'

I had a mass murder scene off Furnace Creek Road and three dead soldiers at Malpais Mesa. Were the two sites connected?

What about Scott Huddelson?

I also had to answer my original question: where is Wally Snyder?

The last problem was keeping the news out of the papers, off TV, and out of the public's eye.

It helped that the FBI and the Army, along with the State of California all wanted to keep the wraps on the Death Valley discovery.

Chapter 17

Two nights after the grisly discovery near Furnace Creek Road, Edith and Alex were having dinner at a local hangout previously known as The Cowboy Bar & Grill. The restaurant and bar was now called The Western. Edith ran her unshod foot up Alex's leg under his pants, her silk stocking gliding over his leg. They smiled at each other.

The news that one hundred sixty-one bodies were found in Death Valley brought many people to town, including Grady Bennett, the reporter from the *LA Post*. Grady Bennett was forty-three, blond, blue-eyed, and six feet tall with a chiseled jaw. He was also self-centered and out for himself.

Grady walked inside The Western at nine that evening. Juan Pérez came out of the kitchen and wanted to turn right around and walk back when he saw Grady, but the newspaper reporter saw him.

Grady called out, 'Juan, how are you doing? It's been a few years.'

Juan forced himself to smile. '*Señor* Grady, how are you?'

'Good, Juan.' Grady looked around the bar. 'I see that The Cowboy Bar changed its name.'

Nodding, Juan replied, '*Sí*, the bar changed the name when I became the new owner. *Señor* Cobb and *Señor* Fowler from the sheriff's office helped me buy the bar after *Señor* Darren Harris was arrested in Mexico for all the robberies in Lone Pine.'

Grady raised an eyebrow. 'I didn't hear about the capture of Mr. Harris.'

Juan shrugged. 'It happened after you left town, *Señor*.'

'Any news since the Hanging Murderer story?'

'No, *Señor* Grady, everything in Lone Pine is quiet as a church.'

'I heard a rumor in LA about finding some bodies up in a cave near Death Valley?'

Juan's face became blank. 'News to me, *Señor.*'

'Can I get a drink in your bar, Juan?' Grady asked.

'*Sí, Señor* Grady, *mi hija* Maria will be glad to serve you.' Juan called to his daughter, 'Maria, *una bebida para está pendejo,* Señor Grady.'

Maria replied, '*Sí Padre*; what will you have, *Señor* Grady?'

Grady smiled at her. 'Bourbon on the rocks will be fine, Maria.'

Maria made the drink for Grady while Juan circled the seating area to find Edith and Alex. '*Señorita* Edith, Grady Bennett just came in,' Juan said.

Edith asked, 'Juan, is the asshole sitting at the bar?'

'*Sí, Señorita* Edith.' Feeling his duty complete, Juan returned to the kitchen.

Edith tapped the top of Alex's hand and walked over to the bar and stood behind Grady. Smiling, she called out, 'Maria, I'll have what Mr. Bennett is having.'

Grady turned around when he heard his name mentioned. He saw Edith, his smile radiating as if she'd waited at this bar for him to return for five years. But he had left Edith, when the story was complete, and had carried on as a gossip columnist, still waiting for a big break.

Maria put the double shot of bourbon in front of Edith. She held the glass up to her nose and smelled the contents before she said, 'Back in town to write another salacious expose of Lone Pine, Mr. Bennett?'

Shaking his head, Grady said, 'No, Edith, I'm here as a reporter for the *L.A. Post* to tell my readers about the bodies that have been found in the Malpais Mesa area.'

'Well, Mr. Bennett, I think that you should take your tawdry self back to Los Angeles before the end of today. Go and crawl around with the phony people you write gossip about, and the information you've written about since the last time you were in town!' Edith threw the bourbon in Grady's face.

Grady still wore his misplaced smile as he wiped his face with his hand. 'Edith, you should know better than that. I will not be coerced out of town by the misinformed and uneducated. I have free speech and the Constitution on my side.'

Alex stood next to Edith. 'If asking politely isn't enough to get you out of town, then how about this?' Alex swung a right-handed haymaker into Grady's face. The blow cold-cocked the newspaperman breaking his jaw, as he fell to the floor, unconscious.

Edith watched, startled, as Grady fell to the floor. Turning to Alex, she threw her arms around his neck and kissed him passionately. Giggling, she pulled away and said, 'My hero. A little more of that, and I might think of me as your girl, cowboy.'

'Golly gee, ma'am, now I'll die a happy cowboy,' Alex replied, smiling at her.

They both laughed as they walked back to their table.

#

Twenty minutes after an ambulance took Grady to the hospital, Edith and Alex were standing in the living room of her bungalow. Her arms were wrapped around his neck. He held her close, slowly running his hands up and down her back.

Alex asked, 'What was that yahoo at the bar all about?'

'He was a nightmare from a long time ago. Someone I want to forget.' Edith smiled as she gazed up into his eyes. 'The only thing I want to remember tonight is the rest of the night with you, cowboy.'

Alex smiled. 'Well, ma'am, let me show you how a real cowboy treats the only woman in his life.' He kissed her, taking his time, enjoying the scent and feel of the woman in his arms.

Edith rubbed her hands over his back, gently massaging the tired muscles.

Alex came up for air and said, 'This is great, but now let me take you into the bedrooom. Tell me your deepest fantasy. My lips will cover you from head to toe, fulfilling your every desire.'

She was light as a feather as he carried Edith, in his arms and through the door, and into her private inner sanctum. There would be no rest for the wicked this night.

Chapter 18

I arrived at my office. Magnus and Ludo were already working, both with phones to their ears. I picked up a cup of coffee from the breakroom and overheard Marlene holding court with the titillating review of the goings-on at The Western the night before. She told about Edith and Alex having dinner together, and Grady Bennett's return to Lone Pine after a five-year hiatus. I hadn't heard Marlene relish telling of the misadventures of someone like Grady in a long time, not since my father left for Mexico almost five ago.

I discreetly left the breakroom, holding a cup of coffee, without anyone there knowing I had entered. My dad and his lady friend were flying up from Zihuatanejo, Mexico, in another week. What malicious, contrived gossip would Marlene have concerning them?

Magnus and Ludo came into my office as I sat in my chair.

'Jim, we went to Indian Wells yesterday and found out Major Jamison Hayes and Wade Arnold were both out of town,' Magnus stated.

Shrugging, I said, 'I'm not surprised. When I interviewed Wade Arnold, Hayes was already gone, and Wade seemed a little squirrelly about discussing anything concerning his boss. Mr. Arnold has something he's hiding.'

I looked at the two agents, waiting for any insight into my last statement, and found no change in their demeanor. 'Any other news on the cases?'

Ludo replied, 'Dr. Crawley called from the medical examiner's office in L.A. He said all the men who were dug up near Furnace Creek Road were Japanese immigrants with government-issued identification cards. We have ten officers tracking down the surviving relatives and getting information about each victim.'

'Any ideas about who would have executed those individuals?' I asked.

'No, Jim,' Magnus said.

Ludo added, 'We need to find the guy who wrote the letter about seeing the men executed.'

'Wally Snyder,' I answered. 'The brother of the town's pharmacist. I'd best go have another talk with Owen and see if Wally has contacted the family again.'

Before I could leave my office, Red came up to us. 'A call came in from Arlo Chadwick's office in San Pedro, next to the Port of Los Angeles. He is Wally Snyder's boss. The man said Wally's working on the new suspension bridge linking San Pedro to Terminal Island of the Port system.'

'Did he give an address where Wally's living, Red?'

Red handed me the information. I looked at Magnus, Ludo, and Red, and said, 'I'm off to San Pedro.'

The ride to San Pedro would take about three hours, giving me time to think about what to ask Wally. In my mind, the tragedy at Furnace Creek was in good hands with Magnus, Ludo, and Red Fowler.

Chapter 19

The construction supervisor told me that Wally Snyder was an ironworker on the bridge project, but he hadn't come into work that day. He told me where Wally lived, and I went over to find him.

The building was a rooming house, set up for single workers who worked for the construction company. Wally's room was 308. I knocked on the door, and it opened a few inches. I looked at the doorknob and locking mechanism and realized Wally let his guest in. I elbowed the door all the way open. The construction supervisor stood behind me,

I took out my gun and cocked the hammer as I called out, 'Wally, It's Jim Cobb.'

The room smelled like something was turning rancid from the heat.

Slowly, carefully, I walked in. I continued to call Wally's name a couple of times before I saw what I didn't want to find.

Wally was hanging from a hook in a rafter in the closet. His hands were tied behind his back. I asked the supervisor to call the police and pushed some windows open with my elbow. Wally's body was stiff, telling me that rigor mortis was in full swing and that he'd likely died twelve to sixteen hours before I arrived. Who called my office to tell me Wally was working in San Pedro?

The LAPD, the county coroner, and police forensic team all came within half an hour. I spent two hours talking to the police and telling them all I knew about Wally Snyder.

The next morning, I walked into the Lone Pine Pharmacy. 'Owen, we need to talk.'

Owen came from behind the elevated counter and directed me to the same small office at the back of the store.

I was irritable and tired of lies. 'You knew that Wally was working in San Pedro on the new bridge for the last year and a half. Why all the subterfuge about him being missing and drinking again?'

Owen gulped and looked at the floor. 'I'm sorry, Jim.' He adjusted his brace as he spoke. 'It was all Wally's idea. He didn't think that you would take his accusations seriously, and he wanted his exact location kept secret.'

I sighed deeply. 'Wally wasn't hidden. I found him in his rooming house in San Pedro.'

'How is he? What did he say?' Owen asked, looking up at me.

I was exasperated and, without thinking, I said, 'He didn't say anything, he was dead. Someone found him down there, tortured him, tied his hands behind his back, and hung him from a rafter in his room.'

Caught off guard, Owen crumpled. 'No, no, it can't be right,' he pleaded as he started to cry for his dead brother.

I put my hand on his shoulder, pissed at myself for laying the news of the death so matter-of-factly to the sole surviving relative. Getting mad at the family of a victim was unconscionable.

'Owen, Wally, was killed the day before I arrived. I didn't mean to snap at you for not telling me the complete story.' I felt like a complete jackass. 'I'm sorry, Owen.'

Crying as he spoke, Owen told me, 'I talked to him on the telephone a few days ago. He told me he wanted you to see him down there, face to face.'

I replied, 'My office received a call from Arlo Chadwick's office before I drove to San Pedro.'

'It couldn't have been Arlo,' Owen replied. 'Wally said Arlo would be in San Francisco for the week with the architect and president of the construction company.'

I made a note of that. 'Someone found Wally there and killed him. The LAPD is working the case as a homicide. I told the detectives how Wally was witness to the mass executions in Death Valley.'

Owen was still red-eyed as he said, 'Someone, the people behind the killings, were searching for Wally since he saw the executions in 1942. Wally was always looking over his shoulder ever since then. He thought he was safe in San Pedro, working on the new bridge, quiet, alone...but he had persistent nightmares about Death Valley and the fear that they would find him. That's why he sent the letter and the phone call.'

I patted Owen's shoulder, speaking softly. 'Did Wally say who he was afraid of?'

Owen shook his head. 'He never knew for sure who was behind the executions, but he said that the vehicles that brought the victims and killers to Furnace Creek all had the same emblem on the bumpers of the trucks. Wally said it was an arrow pointing up to a circle.'

'Did he have any idea which unit it represented?' I asked.

'He never found out,' Owen replied, his eyes filled with tears.

When I left the pharmacy, Owen was still sitting in the chair in his office, calling his wife. My friend was a wreck, and I couldn't do anything about the situation. I wanted to find a lonely, dark place, and drink until I fell and no longer felt the emptiness in my gut. But that was the old me. Before Conchita. Before the kids.

I knew that to find the person or people responsible for killing Wally was going to be difficult. Driving home in my cruiser, I vowed I would move heaven and earth in my search. I would not stop until I'd brought the killer to justice.

Executive order 9066, the edict from President Roosevelt, saying all Japanese living on the West Coast of the United States were to be rounded up and placed in makeshift camps, out in the desert, and other remote areas, for the duration of the war, was signed on February 19th, 1942. By March, there were Army directed evacuations.

There is never any justification for mass murder. One-hundred-sixty-one men and boys killed, all Japanese-Americans. If the killers had just waited a month...

I didn't agree with the internment camps. If the executive order was to protect the Japanese from white America and the inherent prejudicial racism, we as a country failed the men and boys buried in Death Valley. Of course, that was not the reason. By signing it, Roosevelt failed the country.

Chapter 20

JB drove his 1940 Chevy pickup truck, now with Margarita sitting in the passenger seat, and they traveled from Thermal. They were a couple now, more than seven days together. This was the longest time JB had ever spent with any woman.

He did day jobs to pay for the few things needed, as they drove around Southern California. They spent all their free time having sex in the truck, at a motel, or out in the open air. He hadn't killed anyone since the night he met Margarita.

Margarita was an uncomplicated woman with basic needs for herself. She didn't have goals or dreams. Having had no family, no friends, all she knew in life was the rough work of feeding herself, alone. Margarita wanted to settle down in one place.

This time it was different. Margarita was with someone she picked, not the other way around. She had choices for the first time since she was a little girl in an orphanage run by the Sisters of Perpetual Mercy. The little girl was safe with the Sisters, but the life they led was not in her DNA. The girl didn't exactly know what she wanted in life, but being at the orphanage was not it. She left a week after her fifteenth birthday. That was eight years ago.

Now Margarita sat in the passenger seat, all her meager belongings stuffed into a cardboard suitcase, which rode in the bed of the truck.

JB drove the truck no more than fifty miles an hour. Both windows were down, letting in the dry, hot air. Margarita's blouse was open, and she waved a handmade fan in front of her face. She was barefoot. Her left foot beat to the Mexican music playing on the Motorola radio in the dash. while her right foot reached over from her side of the bench seat and rubbed against the man's thigh. It was hot, but Margarita wanted to touch her man for assurance.

Margarita was antsy riding around with the man. When JB felt her foot on his thigh, he knew that it was time to pull over and satisfy the woman, or there would be no peace before he found a place to rest for the night.

The couple had one problem—no place to stay for any length of time. Living in the truck was getting old, and Margarita wanted a real bed. They settled in Yermo, California. The hot, dusty town was located thirteen miles east of Barstow in the Mojave Desert. They found an efficiency apartment for fifty dollars a month, furnished.

This arrangement quieted Margarita. She smiled from ear to ear. JB was relieved, with less yammering for him to hear.

They made the little efficiency their home.

A week later, around ten in the morning, Margarita had made the bed and was washing the coffee cups while JB drove in search of one of the grocery stores in town. He drove slowly, not wanting any peacekeeping authorities to cast an evil eye on him or his Chevy truck.

A young woman was walking alone on a secondary road, off the main highway. JB stopped his truck to ask directions and found himself with the female as a companion, riding to the store. He hadn't killed anyone since before meeting Margarita, but the urge was strong this morning.

The woman's small talk went unheard. JB was determined to finish what he had started. She hadn't a clue what he wanted to do, but after he offered her five bucks for a quick good time, in a quiet place, she honestly thought her day was looking up.

With the business complete, the woman held out her hand for payment. JB took out his worn leather wallet and handed her the five-dollar bill. Her eyes grew big. The money in her hand meant she could purchase enough food for a week with a few coins left over for a new lipstick.

She went to grab what she thought was her payment, but JB held firm to his half of the banknote. His smile disarmed her for a fraction of a second. She smiled for the last time as he pushed his honed six-inch jackknife into her flat abdomen, just to the left of her protruding belly button. Her weak cry was sucked away into the dry air.

JB looked around, opened the passenger door, and pushed her out onto the desert floor. He still held onto the five-dollar bill. The woman's purse was still on the seat. He emptied it before throwing it on her body.

Whenever he killed, his mind always wandered back to the first killing, the migrant worker who called himself *el jefe*, back in 1936. He remembered stealing the truck and heading to the Central Valley and being free of the abuse of other men. Every kill reminded him of the ecstasy he relished with the first. A similar remembrance occurred with each young girl he took for the taking, until this moment in time.

The first young woman he found was about eight months after killing *el jefe*. JB was Seventeen, working in the Coachella Valley, in the small community of Indian Wells, picking dates on the substantial ranch owned by a retired general, Lucian Richmond Hayes. His family had settled in the valley in the 1880s. The girl, Mexican or Indian and no more than sixteen or seventeen, was hitchhiking to the grocery store. He offered her a ride.

The feeling, hidden deep inside, rose up, overtaking his mind and heart. He didn't want sex, he just wanted to control the life of this unknown individual. He wanted to watch the life leak out of her body as her eyes became glassy and stared off into nothing. Once complete, the body became carrion, and he wanted to rid himself and his truck of the body and get back to what the new day offered.

Her body was discovered in a ditch three days later. Her abdomen had been opened from her pubis to her ribs, and her entrails were pulled outside. JB was near Temecula, at the Vail Ranch when the body in Indian Wells was discovered.

Ah, the days of being free and easy, moving from one job to another, never staying in one place for more than a couple of months. JB was king of his domain. He thought that by looking like everyone around him it would cover his tracks and keep the authorities at bay.

Since his reading skills were at no more than a third-grade level, he never knew about the science of police work. He also didn't know the fingerprints he unknowingly left behind matched several other items found near cast-off bodies around Southern

California, Nevada, Arizona, and even down in Mexico. The Mexican police were actively looking for him, too. But, since none of the law enforcement jurisdictions was able to communicate with one another, the trail of dumped bodies became cold investigations.

JB returned to the little apartment with three brown paper bags full of groceries. Margarita put the groceries away before pushing him onto the bed. She wanted satisfaction before he could eat his lunch.

His disposition had subtly changed, from seeking satisfaction and relieving his urge to kill afterword, as a one-two punch to his ego. Now he found comfort and put off the need to take a life. He thought about this while Margarita slept. His conclusions centered on spending more time with the woman and keeping in check his desire to end a life.

Chapter 21

Three days after I found Wally hanging in his rented room in San Pedro, the preliminary report, filed by the medical examiner in Los Angeles, came into the office.

He had been tortured—almost all the bones in his face were broken from the beating he received; cigarette burns on his extremities, chest, abdomen, and testicles were noted. He was strangled before he was hung, evidenced by a ligature mark below the mark left from the hanging rope.

Wally suffered for several hours before death. The ME set the time of death at three or four in the morning the day before I found him. There was no need to relay any of this information to Owen.

Special agents Magnus and Ludo were sitting in my office when I relayed the information about Wally from the L.A. County medical examiner. I also said, 'Owen told me that Wally noticed an insignia on the army vehicles that transported the Japanese men. The design was an upward pointing arrow into a circle.'

'I'll get the information.' Ludo cleared his throat. 'First, I'll give a call to Fort Irwin and see which military units were stationed there in January 1942.'

'Were there any unit insignia on the Jeep found in the cave?' asked Magnus.

'No markings were on the Jeep found in the cave with the three dead GIs,' answered Ludo.

I looked at the ME's report sitting on my desk. 'Gentlemen, our case is grinding to a halt; the only witness to the execution was murdered.' Rubbing my forehead, I continued. 'Hayes and Arnold, the commanding officer and highest-ranking non-com of the dead soldiers we found, are both missing. The only thing we know is that one-hundred-sixty-one Japanese-American bodies were discovered, interred in a mass grave near Furnace Creek.'

Magnus said, 'Sheriff, we are aware they were executed and buried between December 8, 1941, and the end of the war with the most likely date sometime in 1942 when the internment camps were set up by President Roosevelt. Manzanar was opened in March 1942.'

Ludo had made a phone call while Magnus was adding things up without any clear answers.

Ludo hung up the phone after ten minutes and said, 'The unit with that particular marking was the 57th Field Artillery Brigade, also known as the Iron Brigade, for having fired more artillery rounds than any brigade in the American Army during World War I.' Leaning back in his chair, he continued, 'President Franklin Roosevelt created the Mojave Antiaircraft Range in 1940, and in 1942, renamed the range Camp Irwin, in honor of Major General George Irwin, Commander of the 57th Field Artillery Brigade during World War I.'

'What happened to the 57th Field Artillery Brigade after the start of World War II?' I asked.

Ludo read from his notes. 'September 1917, the 57th Field Artillery Brigade acquired the 121st Field Artillery Regiment and was assigned to the 32nd Division. The 121st Field Artillery Regiment was divided in February 1942; the 1st Battalion was named the 121st Field Artillery Battalion, and the 2nd Battalion became the 173rd Field Artillery Regiment. The 121st Field Artillery Battalion stayed with the 32nd Division and distinguished itself in the Pacific, while the 173rd Field Artillery Regiment went to war in Europe, notably Italy. The 121st Field Artillery Battalion and the 173rd Field Artillery Battalion at Superior became National Guard units in June and July of 1947, as elements of the 32nd Infantry Division.'

I added, 'So what was one unit at the end of 1917, became one unit again in 1947.'

The history lesson left us tired.

I finally asked Ludo, 'Were Major Hayes and First Sergeant Arnold part of the 57th Field Artillery Brigade at Fort Irwin in January 1942?'

Ludo checked his notes. 'No, they were assigned to the 4th Infantry Division of the Oklahoma National Guard in March 1942, but they were at Fort Irwin before their reassignment.'

Magnus said, 'Could Hayes and Arnold have had access to vehicles belonging to the 57th Field Artillery Brigade at Fort Irwin in January 1942?'

Ludo answered, 'Yes, they may have had access.'

'This case is getting hazy with any new information we acquire. Three dead soldiers in a cave, one sixty one dead Japanese-Americans in Death Valley, and the man who started the search tortured and killed in San Pedro,' Magnus stated.

Nodding, Ludo said, 'It seems that the officer and enlisted men who killed the Japanese-Americans had a great deal of good luck on their side, except for the one witness, Wally Snyder.'

'He was the witness outside the military, but I think the three dead soldiers in the cave were also witnesses and lost their lives questioning the orders given,' Magnus added.

'We need to find Hayes and Arnold,' I said.

Chapter 22

I arrived home after a long day, with nothing further developing in the case.

The soldiers found near Malpais Mesa were identified, but why were they placed there? Arnold said Corporal Huddelson knew about the cave after they went to Mexico to retrieve the dead soldiers. The story I got from Wade Arnold was a lie, but still... why there?

The bodies found in the gravesite, near Furnace Creek Road, were believed to be Japanese-Americans who went missing sometime between December 1941 and early March 1942, when all Japanese American citizens were rounded up in California. All the bodies were executed with bullet wounds to their backs or heads.

We did find out that the trucks, which transported the Japanese-Americans, belonged to the 57th Field Artillery Brigade stationed at Fort Irwin on that date. Who oversaw the detail was still unknown.

The exact location of retired Major Jamison Hayes and retired First Sergeant Wade Arnold was also still unknown. No one at the Hayes Ranch in Indian Wells had seen either man, knew where they went or when they will return.

Wally Snyder's murderer was still unknown, and the LAPD had reached a standstill on the case.

I hung my hat on the wall peg next to the front door, finally home and safe from the unanswered questions at the office. The house was quiet for a change. I knew that Conchita had put all the children to bed for the night. I love my kids, but just then, I was too tired to handle their rambunctious natures. I only wanted something to eat and a glass of milk before laying my head on my pillow and falling asleep.

I went to the kitchen and saw exactly what I wanted, a hot plate of pork enchiladas with rice and beans, homemade flour tortillas, and a big glass of milk. Conchita was finishing at the sink. She turned and welcomed me into her arms. We kissed as if she were a lifeline, thrown to a man adrift in an endless sea. I felt safe and loved.

I ate ravenously, and after three glasses of milk and seconds on the enchiladas, I settled back, smiling with complete satisfaction.

I relayed what news I had about the case. Conchita listened, not offering a response until I finished. She didn't propose a single question. She took my hand in hers and took me to our bedroom. Conchita knew that for me to resolve any problem at work, I had to set the issue aside and completely relax. We made love until I was free of any other thoughts but satisfying her.

Sleep came without any roadblocks. I didn't dream or think about the case, thanks to my wife.

I woke up later than usual the following morning, entirely rested from the long hours at work and the case that had me bamboozled. It was Sunday, and the house was quiet. Rosita, Conchita's older sister, had come by the house to pick up the kids.

Conchita came into the bedroom with a cup of coffee and a smile from ear to ear and handed me the cup. She took off her chenille robe before lying next to me, with her head on my shoulder.

Smiling back at her, I said, 'This is a pleasant surprise.'

Conchita looked up at me and caressed my face. 'Jim, we get so little time alone in our own house, with our three boisterous children, who always seem to be underfoot, asking *why* or in need of something.' She kissed my neck. 'I thought today we could find time for ourselves.'

We spent the next hour enjoying each other until we were both physically spent.

She bent down, kissed my lips softly again, and said, 'I've been thinking about everything you told me last night. Jim, find out whatever property Major Hayes or his family owns close to Indian Wells. I think he is hiding in plain sight.'

I knew my wife was the smartest person in the room, and her last statement made perfect sense. Another thought came into my head. Where was the father, General Lucian Richmond Hayes? Was he still living?

Chapter 23

I arrived at the office early on Monday morning. My wife had done everything she could think of to make Sunday the most relaxing, worry-free day I've had in months.

A few minutes after I settled into my chair behind my desk, agents Magnus and Ludo came in with steaming cups of coffee. They both looked tired and hungover, with dark circles under their eyes.

Concerned, I asked, 'Did either of you get any sleep over the weekend?'

Magnus responded first. 'I tried, but the information keeps running over and over in my mind, with the same dead ends we couldn't solve on Saturday.'

'I called every military connection I could think of, and nothing looks right.' Ludo grimaced as he added, 'The people I woke up in the middle of the night now hate my guts and will probably never talk to me again.'

'I honestly hear you both. I seemed headed in the same direction myself when my wife changed everything I was thinking of.'

'What did she say, Jim?' Magnus asked, eager to hear anything that would help them.

'Conchita said we should look at the landholdings Major Hayes, his father, and Wade Arnold own anywhere near Indian Wells. They may be closer to California than Costa Rica. I've already asked Edith to investigate any property owned by the Hayes family. I will ask her to look deeper into anyone related to the Hayes family.'

Magnus was the first to reply. 'I think you have a brilliant wife, Sheriff Cobb.' Before Magnus walked out of my office, he added, 'I'll get the Bureau to find out any other places the Major owns or uses. I may have to use the IRS to check out taxes and the like.'

Agent Magnus was on a mission, and he wouldn't be denied his answers. I felt doubly good that Conchita and Edith had put a burr under his saddle, getting the FBI to search in a new area.

I asked Ludo, 'What was the final story about Corporal Scott Huddelson?'

Ludo thought for a moment. 'The soldier Wade Arnold mentioned, who went to Mexico with him to help return the three deserters?'

I nodded. 'Yes, that guy.'

'The official record from the 4th Infantry Division said Corporal Huddelson died as the division crossed the Siegfried Line, on March 17, 1944. The only thing unusual is that the cemetery has no listing for a Corporal Scott Huddelson. I still haven't heard anything from the family down in the China Lake area, where he was from. It seems the only surviving relative is an older sister who still lives there. Scott died at the age of twenty four in 1944, Allan at age twenty five in 1943, and William at age twenty seven in 1945, all in WWII. Charles, the baby of the family, came back from Korea at age twenty two only to die in a car crash, hit by a drunk driver in 1952.'

'That's a sad story if I've ever heard one. Well, it looks like we need to take a little trip to ask Patrice a few questions about her dear departed brother Scott.'

Even though the case was becoming 'curiouser and curiouser,' as Alice said in her journey *Through the Looking Glass*, there were no answers, but a lot of questions.

I needed to change the course of the investigation, a new direction to look at, and find all the missing people in the mystery.

Chapter 24

The Huddelsons all grew up on their parents' ranch outside China Lake. The ranch was sold off after the death of the youngest living son, Charles, in 1952.

Ludo and I went to see Corporal Huddelson's sister, Patrice Taggart.

Patrice came to the front door, dressed in a work shirt and denim pants. She was about five-eight, slight in build, with gray eyes. Her dull hair was tied up in a ponytail, and she looked worn out, older than her forty-six years. Now a widow, with no children underfoot, loneliness shrouded her existence.

After the introductions, Mrs. Taggart directed us to the living room and a seat on her couch. She sat across from us on an ottoman placed before a large leather wing chair.

I said, 'Mrs. Taggart, we are looking for your brother.'

Confused, she said, 'Which one? They're all dead. They all went off to war and died in the service of their country. Except for Charles, who came back from Korea and died here in 1952.'

'We are interested in your brother Scott,' I replied.

Patrice twitched as if a cold wind had come up and frozen her to the bone. 'What about Scott? He died.'

I asked, 'What was your relationship with your brother?'

'Scott came after the twins; he was the fourth child. Charles came several years later. Scott received a lot of shit from me and the twins, and everyone at school bullied him. We all made him do all the lousy work around here until he went in the Army in '38.' Patrice paused, 'I was the only girl here, other than Mama, and she tried to make him feel wanted and loved, but I think Scott was hit in the head too many times. He was different from the rest of us.'

Ludo said, 'We understand that the War Department sent a telegram saying that Scott was killed on March 17, 1944, as the 4th Infantry Division crossed the Siegfried Line into Germany.

There is no record of his grave in any of the American military cemeteries where soldiers from that battle are buried.'

Patrice said, 'The family was never told which cemetery Scott was buried in, not that we ever had the money to go visit the grave.'

I asked, 'Did your family receive letters from Scott until the telegram about his death was sent?'

'Scott wasn't a writer. I don't recall Mama receiving a letter from Scott after he left Italy in July 1944. He wrote about boarding a ship for someplace. Most of his last letter was blacked out by the Army censors.'

Ludo said, 'Did Scott mention a Major Hayes? Or First Sergeant Arnold?'

Nodding, Patrice replied, 'Yes, he did mention Wade Arnold, if that's who you mean. They developed a close friendship. Mr. Arnold sends a Christmas card every year with money in it. I receive it like clockwork.'

Ludo and I both asked, 'How much money?'

'The amount has gone up, last year it was five hundred dollars. I remember that first Christmas, I guess 1946, Mama got one hundred dollars. After she died in 1953, I received the cards.'

'Does Arnold write anything in the cards?' Ludo questioned.

'The only thing written on the cards is, *For Service to the Country. A Grateful Nation* and signed *First Sgt. Arnold*. Never anything else.'

'What about anyone named Hayes? Anything from him?'

'I do recall that Wade Arnold once wrote that after the war, he was assured a place working on the Hayes' date farm.'

Ludo followed up with, 'Do you know where the date farm was located?'

'I recall Mama saying Indian Wells, if that means anything.'

'Yes, Mrs. Taggart, it does, thank you for all your help,' Agent Ludo finished the interview.

During our drive back to my office, I asked Sam, 'Now, why do you think that First Sergeant Arnold, or better yet, Major Hayes, would send a Christmas card full of money to the family of a dead soldier?'

Ludo shrugged. 'My guess would be a good as your own. Unless they were paying off the family for Scott's disappearance, or his assisting Hayes and Arnold in something nefarious.'

'I was thinking the same thing,' I said, nodding.

'The other thought I had,' Ludo added, 'is maybe Scott is working for Hayes and the First Sergeant. And he is the one supplying the money.'

Chapter 25

S am Ludo and I returned late from China Lake and our interview with Patrice Taggart.

Ludo went into the office to work on a few more calls to
military contacts, and I headed home.

Ludo was betting Major Hayes sent money yearly to the families of the three so-called deserters, too, for ulterior reasons.
After our discussion with Patrice Taggart, we both thought that
maybe, just maybe, Corporal Scott Huddelson wasn't dead
after all.

I drove to the corner to make my turn south, toward home,
and abruptly decided to have another discussion with Owen
about his brother.

I walked into the empty store to find Owen making some late
prescriptions. I saw his head pop up and asked, 'Owen, can I
have a word?'

Owen seemed surprised. 'Yes, of course, Sheriff, be right with
you. Have a seat in the back office.'

I sat in the back room and waited. Owen came in a couple of
minutes later in a rush. 'Sorry to keep you, Jim.'

'That's okay, Owen, I was just resting after a long trip to China
Lake. I came here because I want you to tell me everything
about Wally when he returned to your parents' ranch after he
witnessed the executions.'

'Sure, Jim, sure.' Owen sat at his desk and thought a few
moments. 'It was the last weekend before he had to report to
duty. He had enlisted right after Pearl Harbor. Wally went out
on a camping trip that weekend, alone, in Death Valley. He was
near the Furnace Creek Road and witnessed the executions.'

I nodded. 'Tell me what Wally said after his return home that
morning. Do you recall?'

Owen sat back, remembering that day. 'Wally rode fast into
the corral area. I was out in the barn putting away some tack.

He told me what he saw and asked if he should tell Dad. We both agreed that he should tell our father that very minute.'

He stopped talking.

'Then what happened?' I asked, urging him to continue.

'Wally told our dad, and he sat there thinking about the story, not knowing if Wally had made it up or if it was the truth. Wally was shaking, and I think Dad realized that Wally was scared shitless and believed the story, with one wrinkle.'

Owen seemed to run out of steam at this point until I said, 'Yes, Owen, what did your dad say?'

He took a deep breath and forged on. 'Dad said, 'Since the fucking backstabbing, cowardly Japs pulled their raid on Pearl Harbor, maybe the Army tried some traitors and took them out to Death Valley and killed them.' Wally and I never back-talked our dad, we acted like Father's explanation was gospel and walked off. But neither of us was buying it.

'We followed the newspaper for the next week, but never saw a story about what Wally saw, to say nothing of the government, let alone the Army, being responsible for anything. Then we read about President Roosevelt initiating the Japanese internment camps in February. I went back to pharmacy school, and Wally was waiting to go into the Army. I think he had three days left before he needed to report to the induction station in Independence.'

'Owen,' I asked, 'During the war, did Wally write about what he saw in Death Valley?'

'No, Jim, not a word that I know of. He returned from Europe, and the war, a different man. All grown up, but a lost look in his eyes. He had witnessed the liberation of a concentration camp in Germany. After that, he didn't talk much. Within a year, he'd left the family ranch and traveled around, finding jobs. He'd come home for some holidays and Dad's funeral, but he never said much, and nothing about the war or the time before.'

Owen picked up a pencil from the desk, rolling it in his hands. 'Wally was drinking off and on until he received a call from a friend he had known during the war. A fellow named Arlo Chadwick. He's the civil engineer who gave Wally the job on the bridge...' His voice trailed off.

I asked, 'After Wally heard from Chadwick, what happened?'

'Wally became a new man. He stopped drinking. Cleaned all his clothes and packed them in an old suitcase and drove off. He came by a few times, and each time he was more determined to keep working on the bridge until completion. Then he wanted to stay wherever Chadwick's next job was located.'

'He was happy with a secure job and a bright future. What changed?' I asked frowning.

Owen looked at me sadly. 'That's just it, Jim. He never told me.'

Chapter 26

After my talk with Owen at the drug store, I went home. My father and Delfina were sitting at our dining room table, ready for the evening meal.

My dad, Merrill Cobb, has always been a large man, the biggest kid in school and in the Sheriff's Department. At six-feet-seven, with a full head of wavy hair, now turning grey, my father still had a glint in his eye and urgency in his step. Muscular now, he has trimmed down to two-hundred-thirty pounds due to long walks, less beer, and a full life with a woman at least twenty years younger than his seventy-four years.

Delfina Ruiz was another story; she could be anywhere between thirty-five and fifty-five, sultry, dark-skinned, with black-as-the-night almond eyes, which could look straight through anyone. She never had any children, but her life was a mystery—upbringing, relatives, even where she came from—a small fishing village south of Zihuatanejo, Mexico, but the exact location, debatable.

At five foot seven inches in height, she's a foot shorter than my dad, but taller than most women I've seen from Mexico. Her height and regal posture accentuate her lean body and long toned legs. On the surface, Delfina reminded me of a female panther I had seen in *National Geographic* magazines. Fierce, fearless, determined, and giving no quarter to any person in her way.

Our guests were both dressed in casual sightseeing attire, Delfina in a flowered sun dress with wedge sandals strapped to above her ankle. Her makeup was low-key, nothing distinguishable. Dad wore Levi's, a plaid cotton long sleeved shirt, and cowboy boots. If you didn't know they'd just arrived from out-of-town, they looked like the people down the block.

Since this was Delfina's first trip to the United States, they had spent the last few days touring the Los Angeles area, taking in the sights.

We all sat down together, including our children, and enjoyed the lavish meal Conchita had prepared. Merrill kidded with the twins, Gabe and Tom, while Delfina paid extra attention to Rosie. Loving all the attention, Rosie wanted to do everything just like Delfina.

After dinner, the kids went into the den and played while they waited for dessert. Rosie wanted to stay with Delfina but reluctantly went with her brothers when Conchita told her it was time for the adults to talk. We sat at the table, drinking coffee and digesting the elaborate meal of chicken *mole*. The meal, as always, was delicious. Delfina inquired about the recipe, though she never actually cooked any meals for my father at their home. Merrill and Delfina had a cook and a housekeeper.

I discussed my latest case with my dad while we drank our coffee, with a little Four Roses bourbon as an added kick. My heavy drinking days had ended after the murder of my friend Barton Haskel, back in 1957.

Merrill suggested that I go down to San Pedro in person and talk with Wally's friend, Arlo Chadwick, the civil engineer of the new bridge. I agreed with the thought and planned to drive down the next day while my family took Merrill and Delfina out to Scotty's Castle in Death Valley. The winter was the only time the castle was open since the summertime was too hot for anyone visiting Death Valley.

Conchita called everyone back to the table for dessert, a *dulce de leche* cake. The boys raced to their chairs, tripping over each other in their haste, Rosie would only sit next to Delfina and copied her every move.

After we tucked our children into bed, Conchita and I finished the dishes and cleaned up the kitchen.

Our bedroom was dark when I slipped under the covers. I turned to Conchita to kiss her goodnight

She kissed my neck and whispered, 'Jim, I want another baby.'

I held her close and kissed her. Smiling, I whispered, 'Yes, Conchita, let's make one tonight.'

I knew Conchita had a smile on her face.

Chapter 27

S ince 1946, the FBI had received more than thirty examples of latent prints from eight different states and as many jurisdictions. The fingerprints belonged to a man, never yet identified in any data base, who indiscriminately killed people—young, old, any race, either gender. The crimes included stabbing, strangulation, and asphyxiation.

In 1961, the Mexican Federal Police sent six examples of fingerprints from one assailant, who had apparently perpetrated seven murders in northern Mexico, all in different villages and in three separate Mexican states.

Fingerprints from Mexico matched the elusive murderer who had killed in America from 1946 to 1957 and then reappeared from late 1961 to 1962.

There was no other evidence, only the latent fingerprints, to connect the murderer to the crimes. Forensics had some fibers, possibly related to an old Chevy truck, maybe a 1940 or '41 model. The killer kept two steps ahead of the police by never killing in the same area consecutively. This all changed in late February 1962, when three murders occurred in Yermo, California, within two weeks.

The murders were of three teenagers, roughly from thirteen to nineteen, all Hispanic. Two had been stabbed, and one strangled. They all had been sexually assaulted.

The FBI, San Bernardino County Sheriff's Office, and local police were all on the lookout in the Yermo area. The crimes screamed from the headlines of the local newspapers. For all practical purposes, the police thought they had their suspect boxed in, and apprehension was imminent.

It had been ten days since JB had killed a young woman and discarded her out in the desert on his way to the grocery store. A week after the first killing, he killed two more women, all like the first, young, walking along the road.

JB and Margarita saw all the commotion in Yermo and the surrounding area. The talk in the local bars was loud and angry, and a vigilante mentality was emerging

They had lived in the apartment for four weeks. Margarita became fearful of the hostile atmosphere simmering among her neighbors. She knew that moving away was their safest option. They left early one morning, unnoticed, in their newly acquired, faded green 1943 Dodge truck. The old Chevy was gone, left at the junkyard.

The couple drove up to Lone Pine undisturbed.

Margarita never asked her man what he did when he went out alone. She had her ideas.

Neither ever said how or if they cared for the other. The future was tomorrow, not next week or the coming year. Keeping your feelings bottled up inside was the safest place. If you let them out, into the air, and no reciprocal acknowledgment was heard, then loneliness would follow. Isolation was worse than knowing the truth if the truth wasn't what you wanted to hear.

Chapter 28

My first order of business was another ride down to San Pedro for a talk with Arlo Chadwick. I arrived just before lunchtime as I entered the trailer marked 'Civil Engineer—Arlo Chadwick.' His secretary let him know I had come from Independence. I had called before making the trip.

Within a minute, Mr. Chadwick opened the door, held out his hand, and said, 'So glad to meet you, Sheriff Cobb. Please, have a seat, and call me Arlo.'

Arlo Chadwick was slim at six feet tall. His salt-n-pepper hair gave him an older look than his fifty-two-years indicated, and his bright blue eyes looked like ice in a winter's storm.

I sat in a beat-up metal chair in front of his desk. 'I am here to talk about Wally Snyder.'

'After I was informed of his death, I knew you, or someone, was going to want to discuss what I knew about Wally. I'm shocked and saddened with Wally's murder and how it is affecting his family.'

I asked my first question. 'What was your relationship with Mr. Snyder?'

'Wally and I met while serving in the 407th Brigade Quartermaster Company, Support Battalion, as part of the 82nd Airborne Division. We landed with a glider assault team in Holland during Operation Market Garden.' He shook his head and smiled at the memory. 'We both missed out on the Normandy invasion while sitting in the hospital, me with appendicitis and Wally with a stomach ulcer. We were together in the company since April 1942 through the end of the war.'

'What can you tell me about Wally?'

Arlo let out a long sigh. 'He was a troubled soul when I met him. He had something hidden deep inside him that was struggling to get out. He didn't tell me about it until after the division settled into Berlin in April of 1945.'

Before I asked what it was, a thought occurred to me. 'Did you inform anyone of the information Wally gave you?'

'No, Sheriff, I didn't, Wally didn't want me to tell anyone.'

'Okay,' I already knew the answer to my next question. 'So, what was troubling Wally during the war?'

'Well, Sheriff Cobb, you know...the executions in Death Valley.'

I nodded. 'What did he tell you?'

Grimacing, Arlo told me. 'He said what he saw in January 1942. The soldiers killing the bound men.'

'I received a letter from Wally through his brother Owen, detailing what he saw.' I leaned back in my chair. 'My next question is, what did Wally do until he started working on the bridge in San Pedro?'

Arlo shrugged. 'The best I know, Sheriff Cobb, is that Wally drifted through jobs, never finding anything to his liking. He was drinking a lot during that time, alone in a trailer. We kind of lived our own lives, not keeping in touch. I came back from the war and took advantage of the G.I. Bill, getting a degree in civil engineering at Purdue University.'

I asked, 'When did you and Wally find each other again?'

'It was around '58 or '59. I remembered that Wally's brother, Owen Snyder, owned a pharmacy in Lone Pine and so I wrote Wally a letter and sent it there. Several months later, Owen wrote back, telling me about where Wally was living. I went there and found him in a drunken stupor. I moved Wally in with my family and me in San Diego. It took over eight months to get Wally back on his feet, physically and mentally.'

Shaking his head at the memory, Arlo continued, 'Around the holidays in 1960, Wally became a new man; cleaned up, sober, and with new goals in his life. He put all the demons from his camping trip to Death Valley in 1942 and the rest of his war experiences to rest. It was a struggle, but Wally wanted a new life. He even started going out with a woman from our office. The future was bright for Wally Snyder, or so I thought.'

A look of sadness crossed Arlo's face. He stood up and started pacing around the room.

I was about to ask another question when he stopped and returned to his chair.

Fighting back the tears, he told me, 'In November of last year, I sent Wally to a job our company was completing up near Palm Springs. He was there a couple of days when he called me and said that he saw a man from the execution detail in Death Valley. I drove there immediately and found Wally alone in the dark, in his hotel room sober, but mumbling over and over the words, 'Not again, not again."

Arlo paused and asked, 'Would you like something to drink, Sheriff Cobb?'

'Coffee, black, if you have it.'

'Of course, we do. Where are my manners?' He clicked on his intercom and said, 'Doris, please bring coffee in for Sheriff Cobb and me.'

Within a few minutes, Doris brought in the coffee service, placing it on his desk. without saying a word. She saw immediately how distressed Arlo looked. 'Is everything okay, Mr. Chadwick? Can I get you anything?'

'No, Doris, I was thinking about all the time I knew Wally.'

Doris left the office with ashen color in her face.

Gently, I urged him to continue. 'Arlo, you were telling me about finding Wally Snyder in Palm Springs... go on.'

'Wally was in a hypnotic state. I brought him back to San Diego, where I had a psychiatrist see him immediately. The doctor told me Wally had suffered a flashback to an incident in his past that was overpowering his usual, everyday psyche. The doctor visited three times a week for over a month until he seemed back to his old self. The doctor even suggested the idea of hospitalization. He even rekindled his relationship with Doris—she was his girlfriend. Within three months, Wally looked and acted like his former self, how he was before he went to Palm Springs.'

Arlo frowned and ran his hand through his hair. 'Everything was fine until about three months ago, when he had a dream. He told me after, the nightmare wanted him to clean his soul of what he saw and tell the proper authorities—the Sheriff of Inyo County. That was when he wrote the letter to Owen with the request to pass the information on to you.'

I looked at Arlo with confusion before I said, 'Why didn't he come into my office and tell me his story?'

With a sad smile, he answered, 'He was afraid of returning to the spot where he saw the executions. Wally thought that if he stayed away from the area, he would gain strength to fight off his nightmares.'

I watched him closely as I said, 'Owen told me that Wally was hiding in some trailer, drinking his life away, not here working.'

Arlo nodded. 'That was what Wally, Owen, and I decided to tell everyone. It was to keep Wally safe from the people who committed the crimes.'

'We found the burial site and the bodies where he described them in his letter. Why stay hidden then?' I asked.

'You have to understand, Sheriff...' Arlo paused, looking for the right words. 'Wally was still very skittish about the subject. He withdrew from his work at the bridge site and just sat in his room, in the dark. Owen and Doris and I, all of us were worried. Wally told us all to not worry, and that after arrests were made, he would emerge. Unfortunately, sadly, Wally took his own life.'

'Well, Arlo, that's the rub of all this deception. Wally Snyder did not kill himself; he was murdered.'

'What do you mean, *murdered*?' Arlo was shocked. 'Was it the people he was hiding from, Sheriff?'

'I believe so,' I answered. 'And I'm going to find out who killed Wally. Now, I need to talk to your secretary.'

Chapter 29

I spent the next two hours interviewing Doris Murphy, Arlo Chadwick's personal assistant, and Wally's girlfriend. Doris and Wally started seeing each other in early 1960, right after Wally began working for the civil engineering firm where Arlo Chadwick was a partner.

Doris, a bright, energetic, willowy woman, five-feet, five, 32, with raven black hair, fair complexion shining through her cover girl looks, corroborated Chadwick's story of Wally doing well until he went to Palm Springs last November. The only change was that Wally initially called Doris, who told Chadwick, and they both went to Palm Springs together. Doris couldn't talk with Wally. He mumbled to himself in the darkened room, just as Chadwick had related. Almost a hypnotic or fugue type of state.

Doris helped bring Wally to Chadwick's family home in San Diego, where the psychiatrist treated Wally for over a month. Then Doris and Wally returned to her apartment in San Pedro. Everything was fine until two weeks after the couple returned to the job site, when Wally noticed a white 1960 Ford Fairlane 500, a four-door hardtop. He recognized the car from the twin head-lights in the scalloped-square front. She told me Wally knew his vehicles.

Doris said that she saw the Ford after Wally pointed it out. The car was parked down the street from her apartment. After work, the car was across the street from the office. This continued for two weeks. Finally, Wally went back to his rooming house, and three days later, he died there. She never saw the car again.

I asked her if she saw the license plate. She replied that it looked like all the other license plates. She thought a few moments and then told me that there was one letter followed by five numbers. I knew immediately she was talking about a commercial plate, the kind used for all trucks, pickups, delivery vans, and taxis.

Doris then remembered that the letter on the plate was a G followed by 64 and three more numbers; this insight narrowed the search down to a government vehicle.

I confirmed that Wally was murdered. I wasn't sure if the person in the Ford had anything to do with his death, but I've never believed in coincidences in police work, and my inner self kept telling me I was right this time, too.

Doris couldn't remember anything else about her time with Wally before his death. She cried and asked for Owen's address and phone number up in Lone Pine. She blurted out, 'Sheriff Cobb, I'm carrying Wally's baby, it's due in September.'

'I'm sure the Snyder family will want to make you and your baby part of their family,' I said

My thoughts on the drive back to my office in Independence revolved around the feeling I had about who was in the white Ford. One person or more? Did the vehicle follow Wally to San Diego with Arlo Chadwick and Doris Murphy, and then go on to San Pedro? Why did the killer wait until Wally left Doris's apartment before killing him? Thank God he did. If the killer was part of the executions in Death Valley, then why wait until now?

My mind was working overtime. Had the killers from Death Valley been looking for Wally all this time until fortuitously they found him under their noses in Palm Springs? Was Wally in the wrong place at the wrong time? Twice?

Always taking the part of devil's advocate, was there a possibility Arlo Chadwick and Doris Murphy were involved in the killing of Wally Snyder? This last question didn't even have time to settle in my brain before I rejected the thought.

Chapter 30

At my office in Independence, I assigned Edith the duty of hunting for the white 1960 Ford Fairlane 500 with the 'G' government license plates.

I held a progress meeting in the conference room with the dusty chalkboard. I had Red, Perry Rimmer, Carl Magnus from the FBI, and Army CID Agent Sam Ludo in there while I wrote on the blackboard:

1. Three mummified bodies were found in a cave near Malpais Mesa. Later identified as Private Marshall Cox, age Twenty one, Private Harry Crenshaw age Eighteen, and Private William Taylor age Nineteen.
2. First Sergeant Wade Arnold and Corporal Scott Huddelson went to retrieve supposed 'deserters' (Cox, Crenshaw, and Taylor) from Mexico and then placed the bodies in the cave.
3. Bodies of executed Japanese-American men found in Death Valley. Executions occurred between January and (unknown date) in 1942. Most likely before Manzanar was opened in March 1942. The 275th Headquarters Company of the California National Guard at Fort Irwin was on reassignment to the 4th Infantry Division of the Oklahoma National Guard, March 1942.
4. Interview with First Sergeant Wade Arnold at date farm said Major Jamison Hayes was in Costa Rica overseeing family ranch.
5. One week after the meeting with First Sergeant Arnold, both he and Major Hayes went missing.
6. Wally Snyder was sent to a job site in Palm Springs in November 1961 and later entered a hypnotic or fugue state.
7. Wally was brought to Arlo Chadwick's home in San Diego, and with the help of a psychiatrist and his girlfriend, Doris Murphy, became well enough to return to San Pedro.

8. Patrice Taggart, the sister of Corporal Scott Huddelson, was told her brother's body was not in a grave in France. Mrs. Taggart received a card with money from First Sergeant Arnold every year at Christmas.
9. Wally Snyder and Doris Murphy noticed a white 1960 Ford Fairlane 500 with the G 64815 government license plates following them near her apartment.
10. The murder of Wally Snyder in San Pedro was made to look like a suicide, and by hanging.

I finished writing and stood back from the board to check for mistakes when Edith entered and said, 'Jim, the DMV told me the plate belongs to a 1962 Buick sedan used by the State DMV office in Ojai, California. The vehicle was reported stolen in January of this year. At present, there is no new information.'

'Thank you, Edith.'

I wrote on the blackboard:

11. Government license plate G 64815 stolen from a DMV Office in Ojai in Jan. 1962.

I asked Edith, 'Is there any news about other properties that Major Hayes or his family own other than in Indian Wells or Costa Rica?'

'There are seven properties. Four are in southern Mexico, which the FBI asked the Mexican government to investigate, near the border to Guatemala, around the town of Tapachula in the state of Chiapas. The other three are all located in the USA. One in Golden Valley, west of Kingman, Arizona. The other two were here in California. A property south of Indian Wells in the Coachella Valley, a little town called Thermal. The last property has been in the family since 1895, and it's located here in Inyo County.'

'Now we are getting somewhere. Edith, what is the location in Inyo County?'

'Keeler, on the east shore of Owens Lake. Twenty-six miles by road to Malpais Mesa.'

'Keeler, that town sounds familiar; does anyone know anything about the place?'

Red Fowler spoke up, 'Keeler was an old zinc mining town in the early 1900s; a tramway was built, bringing the ore from Cerro Gordo to Keeler.'

Perry Rimmer said, 'In 1950, all the mining stopped. The train stopped running in 1960, and all the tracks were removed in 1961. Maybe fifty to sixty people live out there.'

I asked, 'How do you know so much about the place, Perry?'

'My great-uncle still lives out there.'

Red said, 'I guess we know who is going on a field trip to Keeler.'

Deputy Rimmer, always ready to take on any assignment, was grateful for the chance to get more work than digging up bodies in Death Valley. A trip to see his uncle was a godsend.

Chapter 31

The Cowboy Bar & Grill changed its name to The Western after the Hanging Murders were solved, and Darren Harris was arrested for involvement in the robberies of Hollywood people filming in Lone Pine.

Juan Pérez, the longtime cook at the restaurant, was able to buy The Western with the help of Jim Cobb, Jim's father Merrill, and Red Fowler as silent partners. A Mexican owning a bar and restaurant frequented mostly by white customers in California in 1962 was still a rarity. But Juan, his wife Carmen, and the rest of the family made it work by letting all the people coming in always think Darren Harris or someone else owned the restaurant and bar.

It was a few minutes after six in the evening, and Merrill was finishing his second beer of the day when Red Fowler walked in. These two men had known each other since childhood and had worked together at the sheriff's office for more than thirty years.

Red sat on the barstool next to Merrill and said, 'I'll have a beer, Juan.'

'*Sí, Señor* Red. How are you tonight?'

'Juan, I'm hot, overworked, and thirsty.'

'Good, *Señor* Red, thirsty is good.'

Merrill held his glass up. 'I'll have another, too, Juan.'

'*Sí, Señor* Sheriff.'

Juan served the beers and walked down to the other end of the bar to help another customer.

'Well, Merrill,' Red sipped his beer. 'you wanted to talk; let's go find a quiet table away from anyone walking in.'

The two men retreated to a table and sat down.

Red set his beer on the table and leaned back into the booth seat. 'I'm all ears, Merrill, what do you want to talk about?'

'I want to tell you first. I'm going to ask Delfina to marry me and spend half the year up here and the other half down in Zihuatanejo.'

Smiling, Red said, 'Congratulations, Merrill. It's about time, isn't it?'

'Yeah, Red, it is.' Merrill answered, laughing, 'Delfina and I have been together for the last four years. She has no family left in Mexico, and she's hit it off with Jim, Conchita, and the kids up here.'

'Does Delfina know about Marlene and the other women you were with up here?'

Merrill nodded. 'Yes, I told her right off the bat about my life here while I was sheriff.'

'Everything, Merrill? All the women?' asked Red.

'Yes, Red, every woman. I also told her about how I hurt Clara all those years.'

'And...' Red studied Merrill's face. 'She's okay with all of that?'

Merrill paused a moment. 'Well, she said yes, but Delfina had to know that there would be no other women in my life, or she would leave me.'

Laughing, Red replied, 'Finally, a woman who laid it on the line. Good for her.'

'No, good for me,' Merrill said.

The two men sipped their beers.

'I'm happy for you and Delfina.' Red glanced around before continuing, 'There is one person in town who is not going to be happy, though.'

Merrill shrugged. 'How is Marlene?'

'She was terrible after you left town, saying all kinds of things about you, Jim and Clara.' Red grimaced at the memory. 'Every nasty, derogative, hurtful thing she could think of about women and men in general.'

Nodding, Merrill replied, 'Marlene always had a way with words, especially when it came to her own prejudices toward others, and when she thinks she has been put second in line.'

'Merrill, there is nothing like a woman scorned.'

'Yes, Red, I know. Marlene never accepted not being first. She hated Clara and me for not divorcing back in '26. I didn't treat Clara or Marlene right. Back then, I was a selfish man. A man who never knew what he had or how to treat the women who loved him.'

With a bemused smile, Red replied, 'Sounds like you have learned more than you bargained for down in Mexico.'

Merrill returned the smile. 'I learned about myself and found a woman who won't put up with any shit from an old man like me.'

'What does Delfina do for you?' asked Red.

Merrill took a long sip of his beer. 'She is real, direct, and the best lover I have ever had in my life.'

'Sounds good, Merrill. How do I find what you have?'

'Red, you're ready to retire. Come down to Zihuatanejo. Delfina knows people who can make your life worth living in a quiet fishing village.'

'It sounds just like the life I need.'

The two old friends sat and drank their beers silently, thinking about their own lives.

Finally, Red said, 'Merrill, the life you have in Mexico sounds great. Maybe after I finish with this case we are working on; I might just come down to paradise and take you up on your suggestion. I'm a lot younger than you, and I deserve someone for myself.'

They raised their glasses. 'Cheers.'

Merrill knew that by asking Red to come down to Zihuatanejo and having Delfina working as a matchmaker, his life would be complete. A friend nearby. A wife in his bed. What more could an old codger ask for? Life was good.

Chapter 32

I always enjoyed getting into the office early, before anyone else on the day shift.

I walked in the front door, and before I made it three steps, Marlene Chambers marched out of the breakroom and stood toe-to-toe with me.

Marlene's face was red, and she demanded through clenched teeth, 'What the fuck is your father doing here, flaunting a Mexican whore in public, and acting like he deserves to live among decent white Christians?'

'Marlene, you have just gone over the line. Whatever conflict you have with my father is long over, and you should get over your hostility or find another pulpit to preach from.'

'Don't you talk to me like that, Jim Cobb. Your father is an unconscionable heathen who does not have a right to be in any God-fearing place like Lone Pine.'

'Marlene, the last time I looked, we live in an integrated society where all people are equal under the law-'

She interrupted me. 'It is against the law for people of two different colors to marry in the United States. I should call the District Attorney to lock your ass up right now. Your father should be put in solitary confinement for life.'

I said, 'The California Supreme Court in 1948 reversed the law, allowing any two people of different races to marry. Marlene, you are a little behind the times on this matter.'

'Well, it is against the will of God.' She stood straight and tall as if this would make me see the error of my ways.

But sleeping with married men isn't? I thought to myself.

As if she heard my thoughts, she spat, 'White people should only be with other white people.'

I looked with pity at this misguided person who had grown up in a world that no longer existed. She had become a poor excuse for the ideals of the Constitution, or God. A woman scorned in a love triangle with my father and any other woman he was sleeping with.

Marlene looked like she had steam coming from her body, like a boiler ready to blow. There was no reasoning with her. Her rant was viral in nature, without a cure in sight. What Marlene preached was not going to happen. People had a right to live their lives with whomever they wanted.

Shaking my head, I walked away before she found her second wind in a fight she was never going to win. People were starting to arrive at the office, and I didn't want her rant to become a spectator forum.

I realized that I should have let Marlene go years ago. But her latest display of insensibility would have to wane, or it would look like I was heavy-handed in my actions.

Taking a deep breath, I waited for a moment and called Edith into my office. 'Put out an APB to find Major Jamison Hayes, First Sergeant Wade Arnold, Corporal Scott Huddelson, and any other men still living who had been assigned to 275th Headquarters Company of the California National Guard at Fort Irwin in 1942.'

There was also a 'Be on the Lookout' for the white 1960 Ford Fairlane 500 with the G 64815 government license plates.

Something had to hit soon. The case was slowing down, and that meant finding the people responsible for the mass executions, the dead soldiers, and Wally's murder was getting harder.

Edith handed me a new notice from the FBI about a killer who drove around in an old Chevy pickup truck. Stapled to the announcement was an update detailing a new vehicle, the Chevy was traded in at a junkyard outside of Yermo, for a 1943 Dodge truck in a faded dark military green color. The junkyard owner told the FBI that the disheveled man with a beard was now traveling with a young Mexican woman in her twenties.

I sat back and thought about how my day had started out real fine, and then I came to work: Marlene's racist rant, and the news about the serial killer now having a new truck, and an accomplice.

I can't do anything about Marlene and her ideology from the past.

But the idea of a man who has been indiscriminately killing people for over twenty years. This is beyond anything I could have imagined in my wildest nightmares. I knew I needed to place myself between my county and this murderer.

My fears didn't only entail the people I serve, but also my family—my wife, children, my father and his future bride—plus the many co-workers and friends I cherish, depend on, and love beyond any measure. If anything happened to any of the people I care most about, I don't know how I would react, but I know I wouldn't want to be the first person I came across. I could revert to a wild animal and tear them limb from limb. Like when I went cold turkey for my drinking problem before I heard about the murder of Barton Haskel. I may not be the writer of love poems or sing about my true love, but I never set a goal which looks beyond what any man could do in front of me. I have the grit, determination, and inner passion for successfully accomplishing my goal.

I wanted peace and quiet, harmony among all people in my county, my father and his girlfriend to find their own happiness, and my family to be safely away from all harm.

My hopes for the day returned when Perry called in from Keeler, the defunct zinc mining town his great-uncle lived in. Perry's information might turn this whole case on its ear. Thank God for the decent people who live in our little communities.

Chapter 33

Perry Rimmer drove out to his great-uncle's house in Keeler in his own car, and wearing civilian clothes. Perry's last visit to his uncle had been about six months before. From what Perry said, it seemed that everyone in Keeler looked out their windows at anything that moved—animal, mineral, or vegetable.

I was in my office going over the latest reports from the FBI on the multiple murders committed by the man in the truck.

Edith buzzed my intercom. 'Jim, Perry Rimmer is on the phone from Keeler.'

'Great.' I picked up and said, 'Perry, give me some good news.'

'Sheriff, my uncle says that there were a lot of people going in and out of the Hayes ranch for about two months, but in the last couple of weeks, no one's home.'

'What did your uncle see?'

'Nothing really, Sheriff. Everything he knows he heard from Mrs. Haywood, the eighty-year-old woman who lives on the only road out to the Hayes place.'

'Okay, Perry, what did she tell your uncle?'

'Sheriff, I'm at Mrs. Haywood's house now, let me put her on the phone.'

A soft, demure voice said on the phone, 'Is this Sheriff Cobb?'

'Yes, Mrs. Haywood, it's gratifying to talk with you today. Deputy Rimmer told me you saw people going in and out of the Hayes ranch.'

'Why, of course, Sheriff. Anyone, man or beast, must pass by my place to get there. I keep my eyes wide open for any varmints crossing my path.'

'I would like it if you could tell me what you saw, Mrs. Haywood.'

'Yes, Sheriff Cobb. It started about six months ago when several large trucks came in and out of the Hayes ranch in the middle of the night.'

'How many trucks and for how long?' I asked.

'It was four trucks at a time. All were large hauling trucks, maybe twenty-four feet long, like moving vans.' She paused, and I heard a rustling sound like she was looking through pages in a book or something. 'They came in on Tuesday and left on Thursday each week for three weeks. I mentioned this all to Buster.'

'Who's Buster, Mrs. Haywood?'

'Why, that's Perry's uncle, Sheriff Cobb.'

'I'm sorry, Mrs. Haywood, go on.'

'The trucks came like clockwork, in on Tuesday and out on Thursday for three weeks, then they stopped for a month and started again for another three weeks. This continued for four months. The last two months, nothing.'

I asked, 'Was there anything during the day?'

'No, just at night. I would tell Buster about it when we would get together. Sometimes, the trucks and the noise would bother us.'

'I understand, Mrs. Haywood. Did you or Buster see anything else out there going to or from the Hayes ranch?'

'Yes, Sheriff Cobb. After the trucks stopped, a white car would drive out to the ranch every couple of days in the early afternoon. The vehicle stayed for a couple of hours, then left. This continued until four days ago. Now nothing. The ranch looks deserted. No movement, no lights, nothing.'

'Mrs. Haywood, do you know what kind of white car visited the ranch?'

'I don't know any car makes, Sheriff, but the car did have two lights in front next to each other like eyes, and the taillights were big and round. I think it had four doors, too.'

'Thank you, thank you, Mrs. Haywood, you have been a great help in our investigation. Can you put Deputy Rimmer back on the phone?'

'Here he is, Sheriff.'

I could hear her give the phone to Perry and walk away.

'Sheriff Cobb, it's Perry here.'

'Perry, good work. I want you to stay at Mrs. Haywood's house. I will get a search warrant and send out teams of the CID, FBI, and our own people to help you look through the Hayes ranch.'

'Yes, Sheriff Cobb.'

I hung up and called out to Edith to find Carl Magnus and Sam Ludo. Edith came into my office and asked, 'Anything else, Jim?'

'I need a search warrant for the Hayes ranch in Keeler; find out if Judge Zimmers is in his office.'

The day was proving to be more useful than I first thought. My mind was full of what was out at the Hayes ranch:

What were the trucks hauling?

Was anyone living at the ranch now?

Where there any secret exits from the ranch?

Where were Hayes and Arnold?

Who was driving the white Ford?

Was Corporal Scott Huddelson alive, and if so, where was he?

Chapter 34

The wheels were set in motion. Thanks to a warrant from Judge Zimmers' office, the forensic teams and several officers from the FBI, CID, and Inyo County were on their way to search the ranch in Keeler. I was taking care of paperwork at my desk when my intercom sounded.

Edith said, 'Dr. Crawley from the medical examiner's office in L.A. is on the phone.'

'I'll take it, Edith.' I pushed the appropriate buttons. 'Mark, glad to hear from you, what's the latest news on the execution victims?'

'The medical examiner's office has finished with the one hundred sixty-one victims. Let me give you the breakdown. I have already sent a printed copy to your office.'

'Go ahead, Mark.'

'One hundred sixty-one male victims, all with gunshot wounds entering the back of their necks or backs. Forensics found multiple rounds in some of the bodies. All in the backs of the victims, and the surrounding area of the grave. All the victims had wounds consistent with a .45 caliber automatic pistol.'

I interrupted the technical jargon from Dr. Crawley and asked, 'Were you able to find out who the victims were?'

'Yes, Sheriff. A wallet was found on each one, with their identification cards inside, so we've made a positive identification for all one hundred sixty-one victims. The dead ranged from nineteen to fifty-eight in age. Ninety-two were born in the United States, and all the others emigrated between 1908 and 1915. Eighty-eight lived in Los Angeles County when they went missing; twenty-three from Riverside County, thirteen from Orange, twelve from San Diego, and twenty-five from Imperial County. All the men disappeared between December 18, 1941, and February 16, 1942.'

I wrote this information down as fast as I could. 'What else?'

'The families of each victim had notified the authorities about the disappearances. The local police turned the missing person cases over to the FBI. The FBI never found any witnesses who saw the abductions, but some people remembered seeing military trucks driving around the locations where the men disappeared. All the cases remained open until the bodies were discovered. None of the victims had any negative history with law enforcement.'

'That answers a few questions,' I said.

Dr. Crawley added, 'Oh, Sheriff, when the FBI looked into the missing men, they found that all had disappeared either early in the morning when the men went to work or at night when they should have returned home. The families never understood how their loved ones just disappeared until now.'

I admitted, 'We are trying to find the military personnel who were involved with the three bodies found in the cave. We have APBs out, but as of today, no news.'

Crawley replied, 'Speaking about those three dead soldiers, they were shot with .22 caliber rounds that remained inside their skulls. The bullets all came from the same weapon. The one interesting finding was that the stomach contents of each man consisted of ham and eggs.'

'Did the families claim the bodies?'

'Yes, they did, all to different mortuaries in four separate counties.'

Nodding, I said, 'Sounds like you've been busy on this.'

'We have been, for sure. I also sent the final report on Wally Snyder, found hanging in San Pedro, an apparent suicide. He was strangled first and then hung. He sustained a ligature mark on his neck, separate from the rope. I ruled it a homicide.'

'I never thought it was suicide after talking with the family, his employer, and his girlfriend.'

'The LAPD will keep you apprised of any new developments in the case.'

'Thanks, Mark, for all your help.'

'My pleasure, Jim.' We hung up. I went out to the chalkboard to add the latest information.

Information was excellent, but finding the people responsible was difficult. I was leaning more and more to Major Hayes and First Sergeant Arnold as the major players behind the killing of the one-hundred-sixty-one Japanese men and boys.

It was turning out to be a productive day. Even though I had more questions.

Chapter 35

J B and Margarita were on their way to Inyo County when he thought of someone living in an obscure little town in Kern County near where California routes 14 and 58 intersect. He left Rte. 395 just north of Edwards Air Force Base, a 470-square-mile installation that encompassed all the land between routes 14 and 395 in California's high desert. He traveled west of Rte. 58.

The 1943 Dodge didn't go fast on the two-lane road. The heat of the high desert was already pushing past ninety degrees at eleven o'clock in the morning. Both windows were down. Margarita had her small bare feet resting on the dash, and her full cotton skirt was pulled up, showing the man a hint of her lace panties. Fanning herself with a throwaway advertisement of houses in the area, she said, 'It's too hot to drive. Pullover.'

JB saw a dirt outlet track up ahead to the right. He slowed and followed the course at speed just above idling. He stopped the truck some two hundred yards from the asphalt highway. The Dodge faced away from the road. The sound of the few passing vehicles became unrecognizable white noise to the lovers. They were panting from the physical exertion, their sweat making their thin cotton clothes stick to their glistening skin. They were one at that moment, nothing else existed or mattered.

JB was never happy with his life before finding Margarita, never having anyone who loved or cared about him. His life contained only times when he satisfied himself, either killing or having sex with unknown women. The killings were something he needed to do. He didn't care about the person, just that his desire to kill started deep down. His appetite to feel someone else's blood slide between his fingers as their life slipped away was a sensation that began deep in his bowels before it rocketed past bone and sinew, tasting bitter and vile on the back of his tongue. He had to feed the need, or he would go mad. Once satisfied, he could go days without the internal demon rearing up in his mind, forcing fulfillment, or his worse fear, his death.

They arrived at the little restaurant that the man remembered. The lunch crowd was long gone, and the dinner patrons had yet to enter.

The waitress, filling the salt and pepper containers, was the same woman JB remembered, she wore her uniform, a yellow dress with white trim. She saw him and gave a smile. She then saw Margarita and offered a broader, approving smile. The waitress slid into the booth, next to JB, she whispered in his ear. He put his hand on her ass and squeezed. Margarita smiled at the other woman and licked her lips, signaling a hidden desire.

The waitress took their orders and came with the food, iced tea, and the key to her little house. She told them she would get there in an hour. Both he and Margarita smiled approvingly.

Over the next three days, the three never left the woman's bed except to relieve themselves. There was enough to drink, and when they felt hungry, the woman called the young boy from the restaurant to bring them food. On the last night, the boy stayed, and the four frolicked throughout the night. Afterward, they slept in the arms of whoever was nearest.

JB hadn't killed anyone in almost a month. He needed to feel that power. His time was coming soon, just a few miles up the road.

The few days in Mojave were excellent, with food, drink, and sex aplenty. But the gnawing started deep down in the secret place, the place he couldn't understand existed until the feeling rose up and made itself known. It kept repeating in his head, starting with a low grumble and edging up to high pitch—*find someone along the road, alone and vulnerable, ripe fruit for the picking. Prey to be taken at will. Watch life leave them as the inner joy erupts through your body, causing the ultimate satisfaction.*

Chapter 36

J amison Hayes was born in 1896 to Lt. Lucian Hayes and his wife, Mathilda.

The year he turned five, the family moved to the Philippines, where his father had been deployed.

Lucian and Mathilda arrived in the Philippines in 1901. Jamison in tow. The little tyke was up to the heat, crowds, and unusual food, and the boys' school was on the base, with American teachers. There was little interaction between base personnel, their families, and the local people. Jamison lived a sheltered life for the six-year tour his father endured.

Lucian was promoted to captain upon his return to America in 1907, and a posting to Fort Bliss in Texas. The Fort had been in existence since before the Civil War, but in 1891 the new location, on La Noria mesa, was laid out and in 1893 became home to the 18th Infantry.

Next came Camp Benning, in Columbus, Georgia, on the border with Alabama, there since its creation in 1909. The base had served as the home of the Infantry until 1911, when Lucien and his family arrived. During their stay at the sprawling post, Lucien received a promotion to Major. The Army and the Infantry were good for Major Hayes.

Jamison grew up alone. The friends he did make, few and far between, all wanted to relive the Civil War. All over the South, towns and states started to erect statues of Confederate war heroes and leaders. The boys were all sons of officers like his father, some with higher rank, and others lower. They all wanted to live in an America where white men ruled society, government, wives, and families. A lesson learned at home and the schools on base.

The move to Camp Benning as Jamison turned fifteen was a watershed moment in his life. School on the post had boys of officers separated from enlisted children. Playing baseball took on the War between the States, with everyone wanting to be on the Confederate side.

The United States, in 1911, was a white nation. Segregation of the military, separate bathrooms and water fountains for whites and people of color. Jim Crow laws, poll taxes in the South, and even in some places in the rest of the country. Many communities dedicated Confederate generals as war heroes and erected statues and monuments. The country was divided; whites, and everyone else; even women didn't get to vote for nine more years. White men ruled a land of themselves.

Jamison found out this subtle truth through bullies at school, watching the attitudes at Camp Benning, and any surrounding 'camp' towns. The colored, located, at the bottom, along with Jews, Asians, Catholics, immigrants, and finally, women. Unfortunately, the prevailing attitudes were pervasive and seemed ingrained in the very fabric of life.

Even the daughters of officers took on old Southern attitudes, with cotillion or debutante balls when the young ladies turned sixteen.

This coming of age was difficult for Jamison. His birthday, so close to Christmas, made him the smallest for his grade. He was shy in front of girls. The bullies in the school, boys in the class above his, were relentless in hazing younger males. Survival meant to do and say what the older and bigger boys wanted.

Relentless attacks behind the schools were commonplace. Black eyes and bloody noses were an almost daily occurrence. So were being made to eat things like cigars, food not fit for pigs, and bugs. It all left Jamison with a cold heart and thoughts of becoming like all the boys he hated. He came to understand he needed to continue the attitudes of the older boys he resented. To stay alive and be accepted, he became what he hated, taking it on as he transition to adulthood.

The Army segregated soldiers. Camp towns divided by race. Talk filtered down about the lynchings of black men and women, with pictures of town folks looking on.

Bullies helped mold Jamison into an arrogant, selfish, self-centered male. He learned to pick out the weak younger boys and make fun of the individual's speech, heritage, location

of birth, and religious affiliation. Jamison grew to have an attitude reflecting those of his bullies.

Lucian's next post was the Presidio of Monterey in 1913. A
school of musketry was located at the Presidio from 1907 to
1913. He kept close ties with the leaders of the Infantry at the
Department of War.

Jamison finished high school in June of 1915 and would start
college at West Point in September. Jameson never went to a
school dance, never even went on a date until his sophomore
year at West Point.

Chapter 37

I received the call from Red at the Keeler ranch late in the day, just as I was preparing to get out of the office and head home.

The ranch was deserted, Red said. It looked to the investigative team as if the last person had left weeks earlier. The only significant piece of evidence was a room wholly furnished as a hospital suite. Red gave me all the details of the equipment found and asked, 'Jim, was there a record of a war injury to Major Hayes?'

'I know of the amputation of his left arm, but further than that, I don't know. I'll get Sam Ludo to find out more about Hayes during his military years and anything since his discharge from the Army.'

Red hung up, and I sat at my desk, thinking. Was Hayes physically capable of making a trip to Costa Rica?

When Ludo and I had visited the ranch in Indian Wells, Wade Arnold had never given us any indication that Major Hayes was physically ill or disabled.

I remembered Edith had told me that Major Hayes's father, retired General Lucian Richmond Hayes, was still alive and living in Palm Springs. I had read an article in the newspaper that General Hayes had entertained President Eisenhower nearly three months earlier, in the first or second week of December. Ike played golf at the O'Donnell Golf Club with Bob Hope and Arnold Palmer while General Hayes drove their golf cart. Quite an undertaking for a ninety-year-old.

My intercom buzzed. 'Yes, Edith, I thought you had left for the day.'

'I'm on my way out the door for dinner with Alex at The Western. I want to tell you that Conchita called a few minutes ago, while you were on the phone with Red.'

'Did she say if she wanted me to call? Or just get my behind home?'

'She never said which, Jim.'

'I better call, just in case.'

'Good idea. Goodnight, Jim.'

'Goodnight, Edith.'

I called the house to find out what Conchita wanted. The house phone rang and rang without an answer. Unusual but not unheard of; maybe Conchita and the kids were outside and didn't hear the phone ringing. I put a call into Conchita's sister, Rosita.

The phone rang a couple of times before Pablo, Rosita's husband, answered. '*Hola*, hello, this is Pablo.'

'Pablo, this is Jim. Are Conchita and kids there at your house?'

'They all left a few minutes ago for the hospital. I'm on my way, *también*.'

'Pablo, what happened? Who-?'

'Rosita said Merrill, *su padre*; she didn't tell me why.'

I hung up before Pablo finished and rushed out the door. The hospital was a few blocks away from the office.

I rushed to the hospital to find out what had happened to my father. My mother, Clara, had died from a sudden heart attack in 1956, three months after the car accident that killed my first wife Harriet and our only child, Kendall. The pain and agony of the loss of those three had sent me on a downward spiral into a bottle. If those events hadn't happened, I would never have married Conchita, my wife, and mother to our children.

Merrill had always been a hulk of a man. Too big for anyone to fight. Too career-driven to ever get voted out of office as the sheriff of Inyo County. He and my mother had married in 1911 when he was twenty-three, and I was their only child. He was elected sheriff in 1920 and held the job until he retired in 1955 when I was elected to the position. A Cobb has been sheriff of Inyo County for forty-two years.

My mother did one beautiful thing during the war, she helped bring Conchita Ramirez, Rosita's seventeen-year-old sister, from Mexico to work at our ranch in the Owens Valley. Conchita and Rosita's parents were both dead by 1944; they had no other known family members. From the first day, Conchita Ramirez arrives at the ranch, she admired and was devoted to my mother, Clara.

When Conchita arrived at my parents' ranch, I was a military police captain stationed at Rattlesden Airfield in Suffolk, England. When I returned home from the war, unknown to me, Conchita fell in love with me. After my mother's death, she continued taking care of the house for my father and me.

Eventually, she left the ranch, moved into her sister's house, and waited for me to pull my head out of my ass and realize that she was all there was to life. We married, have three beautiful children, and were given my parents' house and ranch as a wedding present from my father, who had since moved to Mexico and met Delfina Ruiz.

The relationship I have had with my father was distant when I was growing up—he was the Sheriff, and I was just a kid. I idolized him and wanted to grow up and be just like him.

I never saw his meanness until I was about to board a train when I was leaving for the army, and war, in 1943. Merrill shook my hand and said to me, 'Jim, I want to tell you that when you and Barton took the prisoner back to Tijuana in 1941, he bought you that prostitute you spent the night with behind the cantina.'

I can still hear my father laughing at me like it was the best damn joke he'd ever heard. I had watched as he walked back toward town. I boarded the train, hearing that man's humiliating laughter as I went off to war. I hated my father ever since that day.

Yes, I've hated and loved my dad, but since he left Lone Pine for Mexico and a new life, Conchita and I have found the meaning of life for two lost people. Now, as I walked into the hospital, I wanted to have a few more years with him. At seventy-four, my dad wasn't old. Feeling bewildered, I rushed through the emergency doors and asked the first person I saw, a nurse, 'Where is my father, Merrill Cobb?

She pointed and said, 'The third cubicle down. Behind the drapes.'

I ran to the area, expecting to see his dead body lying there alone as I pulled back the curtain. Instead, I saw my dad, Delfina, and Conchita with smiles on their faces, as if it were Christmas morning with tons of presents to open.

When Conchita saw me, she walked around Merrill's bed and took my hands in hers. 'Jim, we thought he had a heart attack, but it was only indigestion. He's okay.'

I was so relieved, hearing the reassuring news. 'That's great news, but I almost drove off the road getting here. Dad, don't scare me like that again.'

Merrill snorted, 'Jim, I'm too ornery to die. Anyway, Delfina and I have too many things we want to do together. Now all of you shoo away. I need to get dressed and get out of this place.'

A false alarm of imminent death was enough to take a few years off anyone's life, and I had too many years I wanted to spend with my wife, children, and future grandchildren. There was also a County Sherriff Department to run. Plus, the case at hand was too big to let go of now; I needed to see it to the end.

Chapter 38

Magnus and Ludo were both drinking coffee when I came in. I nodded good morning, went to get my own cup of coffee, and then we all sat down in my office.

I said, 'We need to go down to Palm Springs and have a talk with General Lucian Richmond Hayes about his son, Major Jamison Hayes.'

The article about General Hayes golfing with President Eisenhower had come out six months ago. When I called, the club related all the pertinent information about the article and the four celebrities in the photo.

The O'Donnell Golf Club was able to give me, as the sheriff, the address of General Hayes's home. The director of the club added that the general was a lifetime member, and one of the First 25, the original members.

We arrived a little after two in the afternoon. The sky was bright-indigo blue, and the temperature was in the upper seventies. A beautiful day for golf, if one was in the mood.

General Hayes lived on a cul-de-sac. The general's house was large and set on a substantial piece of land. There were two other houses, one on each side of the general. Both houses were much smaller than the general's, but each had significant acreage surrounding it.

The general's home was a large Tudor style, at least four thousand square feet, with an adjoining tennis court, an Olympic sized swimming pool, and lush vegetation only paid gardeners could nurture. The grounds looked deserted. FBI agent Magnus rang the bell, which sounded like a carillon.

It took almost two minutes before a small Filipino man named Fernando, somewhere around fifty years of age, answered the large mahogany double doors. His face was clean-shaven, unblemished, a few wisps of gray hair combed across his smooth pate, and he was dressed in a gray coat, white starched shirt, and mauve bowtie. 'Good morning, gentlemen. Can I help you today?'

I responded, 'We want to speak with General Hayes.'

'I'm so sorry, but the general is not receiving visitors today.'

He started to close the large wooden door when Magnus barked, 'I'm with the FBI.' He then pointed to Ludo and me. 'He's an Army CID Agent, and this is the sheriff of Inyo County. We're here to see the general, now let us in.'

The man looked at Agent Magnus with contempt and said, 'The general is indisposed at the moment and cannot see anyone.'

Agent Magnus pushed past the servant as we all entered the large vestibule. Magnus turned to the man and demanded, 'Now, take us to see the General.'

The man had taken orders from rude white people all his life, and this time was no different. He gave in and led us to a size-able ornate master bedroom in the back of the house. The room was dark and musty; cigar smoke hung on us like a fog. The man walked to two large windows and drew back the heavy lined draperies. Dust peeled off the fabric like snow falling in a storm.

On the bed was an emaciated figure, propped in a semi-sit-ting position. We gathered around on the right side of the bed. The man's head was turned to the right in a fixed stare, a line of spittle oozed out of his mouth, and his left hand was contorted in a permanent fist. There was a three-day growth of loose hair in multiple gray-white colors on his chin. His face was wan in appearance. His body couldn't have weighed more one-hundred pounds, with rolls of skin covering the abdomen.

The man's deep blue eyes with gold flakes darted to each of his interlopers, before fixing on the manservant who stood next to the bed. His speech was slurred. 'Fernando, who are these men, and what do they want?'

'General, they are the *pulisya*. I told them that you were not receiving visitors today.'

The old man asked, 'Why? Are they here?'

I stepped up and said, 'General Hayes, we want to know where your son, Major Jamison Hayes, is.'

'My son Jamison is dead, he died a long time ago, before the war.'

'No, General, your son didn't die before the start of the war,' I responded.

'To me, the boy is dead. I will not speak of him. The boy was a dishonor to my name. Fernando, show these intruders the door.'

The servant led us back down the long hallway and said, 'Gentlemen, the general suffered a stroke three months ago, leaving him in the condition you witnessed. I do not expect the old warrior to last much longer.'

Sam Ludo asked, 'What was he saying about his son, Jamison?'

'Sir, after Pearl Harbor, Jamison went on a mission, and once the General found out the specific details, he never saw his son again.'

'Do you or the General know what Jamison did?' Sam asked.

'I didn't know anything, but the General was told by his son the details. The General never told me. The General wept the entire night after Major Hayes left the house. As far as I know the General has not talked with the Major since January 1942.'

'Do *you* have any idea where Jamison Hayes is?' I asked.

'If the major is not at the date farm in Indian Wells, then try the houses next door to this one. That is all I can say. Good day, gentlemen.'

He opened the front doors and bowed as we walked through. I never knew wealth before, and I didn't like its smell.

As we walked out to the car, Magnus said out loud to no one in particular, 'What the fuck was that all about?'

I replied, 'We'd better take a look next door for the evasive major.'

Ludo added, 'I don't ever want to get that old. All the money in the world is not going to make the man's passing any easier.'

Chapter 39

Both houses looked empty. We went to the home to the left of the general's. The house was dark, with all the curtains drawn. There weren't any cars outside, and there was no way to look inside. Ludo rang the bell several times without any answer.

Finding no one at home, we all walked across the street to the third and last house on the cul-de-sac. This house was also dark and closed, but as we got closer, we saw that a gardener was working on some plants in front, near the door. This man looked larger than average, with a muscular upper body, a farmer's tan, and a conical hat on his head to protect him from the harsh rays of the sun.

He stood up and turned toward us as we walked up from the street. His weather-worn face and dark eyes hid any sign of friendship. He wiped his hands roughly on his pant leg.

Magnus held out his FBI credentials and said, 'I'm Carl Magnus of the FBI.' He pointed to us. 'This is Sam Ludo of the Army CID and Sheriff Jim Cobb from Inyo County.'

Shaking hands, the man said, 'I'm Mort Beach. I do all the gardening on the block. What can I help you with?'

Although his hat left a shadow on his face, I could tell that Mr. Beach appeared to be in his late thirties to mid-forties, with crow's feet around his eyes and wrinkles from the sun.

Magnus answered, 'We are looking for the owner of the house. You know where he is?'

'I've never seen anyone in this house, or the one across the street.'

'Do you also do the gardening at the big house?' Ludo pointed to the Tudor. 'General Hayes's place?'

'Yes, I do the gardening for all three houses.' He added, as an afterthought, 'I've never been inside any. The Asian man in the white coat gives me water sometimes. He never says a word, and I don't ask questions.'

Carl Magnus replied, 'Do you know Major Hayes or a Wade Arnold? Hayes would be in his sixties and Arnold a little younger.'

'I've never heard of either name before.'

The gardener was getting a little antsy, probably wanting us to leave him alone. Suspicious, I asked, 'Ever seen or heard of a Scott Huddelson?'

I noticed as I mentioned each part of the name, the gardener gave a little reveal, like a poker player who just received a winning card, but he said, 'No, never heard of that person, either. Anything else, gentlemen? I must get back to work. It's getting late and into the hottest part of the day.'

We started to leave when Sam Ludo turned and asked, 'Where's your truck? The one holding all your equipment. The one you came in?'

The gardener looked at Ludo. 'I don't have a truck. I was dropped off this morning, like every morning, by the boss. The equipment I use is stored in a shed behind the house.'

Ludo pressed, 'What happens when it is time to leave?'

'The boss picks me up at quitting time.'

'What if you get finished early?' Ludo added.

Shrugging, the gardener said, 'I work until the boss shows up. That's all I know.'

Magnus asked, 'Do you mind showing us the shed?'

'No, not at all, but I need to get back to work. The shed is around back,' the gardener said, nodding toward the rear of the house.

I said, 'Okay, we can find it by ourselves. What did you say your name is?'

'Mort Beach is my name.'

Before walking around the back of the house, Ludo asked, 'Do you live around here, Mr. Beach?'

'I live up in Morongo Valley, across the line in San Bernardino County.'

'The boss picks you up each day?' I asked.

'Yeah, he picks me up and drives to the job each day.'

I asked, 'Who's the boss?'

'My brother, Jack Beach.'

Magnus, Ludo, and I walked around the house to look at the storage shed. We had to pass the garage on the way. The garage door had three windows across the top third. Ludo peeked in.

'Jesus Christ, there is a white Ford 500 in there. I can see G 64815 government license plates,' Ludo said.

The roll-up garage door was locked, but the entrance door next to it was open. We all went in, saw the car with the license plates, and immediately realized that we needed to talk with the gardener, Mort Beach.

We rushed out to the front of the house. No one was there. It seemed that Mort Beach had vanished into thin air.

Magnus went back to the general's house, where Fernando, denied seeing the gardener.

I remembered that I had a picture in my car's glove compartment. The snapshot, given to me by Patrice Taggert, was twenty years old, but the man in the photograph was the supposedly dead army corporal, Scott Huddelson.

From General Hayes' house, I called the Palm Springs police, Riverside County sheriff, and the San Bernardino sheriff in hopes of tracking down the probably no longer dead Scott Huddelson.

Roadblocks were set up in the area by the local police. San Bernardino sheriff's deputies went in search of Mort Beach's home in Morongo Valley. Carl Magnus was able to get search warrants for the three houses and any outbuildings on the cul-de-sac.

A short trip to Palm Springs was going to turn out to be a long hard day. I called home to let Conchita know I would be home late, or possibly not until the morning.

If the gardener calling himself Mort Beach was in fact Corporal Scott Huddelson, did Major Hayes or First Sergeant Arnold direct him to work at the General's house? Was the General in on everything?

Who was driving the white Ford 500, with the G 64815 government license plates?

Chapter 40

L ucian Richmond Hayes ended up a two-star general in the U.S. Army before he retired in 1935 at the age of sixty-three. He was born in Indian Wells, California, in 1872.

His parents, Ballard and Florence Hayes settled in Indian Wells in 1870 after emigrating from England. They developed a thousand-acre ranch to grow vegetables but converted it to date palms by the 1890s. They found out that only female plants bore fruit and started a horticultural offshoot on the farm.

Brown-haired, blue eyed Lucian grew up strong and tall, learning to hunt and fish, and taking a young German immigrant, Hans Becker, on hunting and fishing trips. Han Becker's father and uncle owned the Wyman Bank of Palm Springs.

In 1890, Lucian, by then six feet tall, boarded the train for West Point. He met Mathilda during their sophomore year at a coming-out ball for children of well-off English parents in Southern California. It was Christmas, and both were home for the holidays.

Mathilda Squire was a strikingly beautiful young woman with raven-colored hair and violet eyes. She went to the College of Notre Dame in San Jose, California. The school chartered in 1868, the first college in the state of California authorized to grant the baccalaureate degree to women.

The two found each other smart, dynamic, and fun to be around.

In 1894, Lucian graduated top of his class, and he married Mathilda in July right after graduation. Their nuptials held in Santa Barbara, her hometown, at Our Lady of Sorrows, the oldest Catholic church in the area, dating back to 1782.

After a quick, two-day honeymoon, Lucien reported to his first posting at the Presidio of San Francisco.

Their son Jamison was born two years later.

In 1913, when Lucian was stationed at the Presidio of Monterey, he heard about a militia group in Idaho and Nevada, created and run by two men, Horatio Turner, the father, and Kenneth, his son. The father and son owned and ran a silver mine, The Majestic Mine, in Virginia City, Nevada. The Idaho-Nevada militia was one of many offshoot organizations sprouting up over the country, and the Army wanted to know everything dedicated career officers like Lucian could find out.

In the summer of 1915, Lucian and Jamison, who had turned nineteen and was scheduled to start his first year at West Point, went to Virginia City to find the Turners and eventually accompany the leaders to the militia training areas in Idaho.

The Hayes men went to the office of the Majestic Silver Mine in Virginia City, Nevada, first by train to Reno, then horses to the mine office.

The office was quiet as Lucian walked in. A secretarial desk was the first thing to see in the unadorned space. Sitting at the desk was a woman, her hair pinned up off her neck and secured to the back of her head, wearing a white blouse with a high collar and long sleeves. She appeared to be middle-aged, over forty but not fifty. Lucien noticed she was wearing just enough makeup to make any man take notice. A couple of pencils tucked in her pinned-up hair; she was reading something.

Lucian, holding his military hat at his chest, cleared his throat to get her attention. 'Excuse me, we have an appointment with Mr. Turner.'

The thin woman, of medium height, stood up and walked around her desk, her dark navy skirt brushed the top of her button-up shoes. She stood with her shoulders back, as tall as she could muster. Smiling, she said, 'Hello, I'm Mrs. O'Leary, Mr. Turner's secretary. Are you Major Hayes?'

'Yes, ma'am, I'm Major Hayes, and this is my son, Jamison, he's going to West Point this fall. Does Mr. O'Leary work here at the mine?'

'No, Mr. O'Leary has passed on. I'm better off now, working for Mr. Turner.'

'Sorry to hear about your loss. Is Mr. Turner in?'

Mrs. O'Leary waved her hand and smiled. 'Yes, and he's expecting you both.' She escorted them around her desk and opened the door to Kenneth Turner's office, 'Mr. Turner, here are your guests, Major Hayes and his son Jamison.'

After introductions were made, Kenneth took Lucian and Jamison out to dinner at the Silver City Steak House. They each had a two-inch porterhouse, 16-oz cut aged beef, medium rare, and a big baked potato. Lucian and Kenneth imbibed in a port wine after dinner as a tribute to the dinner and their next day visit to the militia camp.

After dinner, Kenneth brought Lucian and Jamison to see a new movie, *Birth of a Nation,* at the town's only movie theater. It was just a short walk across the street to the Silver City Hotel, where Kenneth arranged their room. The General was upset by the theme of the movie and more upset when his son praised the KKK.

The room on the third floor of the hotel had two large beds and a washbasin and mirror. A standard commode and shower were down the hall. The hotel room had gaudy wallpaper with depictions of outdoor scenes. The paper had elevated areas in multiple colors. Lucian and Jamison looked at each other and laughed. 'Son, it looks like a Kansas City whorehouse I visited before I married your mother.'

Jamison had never been with a woman, or near a whore-house. He sat on the bed and said, 'I bet the bed is at least bigger and softer than Kansas City.'

Lucian looked at his son and realized he had never talked to him about the opposite sex or anything about growing up and being a man.

The next morning Lucian and Jamison were eating steak and eggs with potatoes in the hotel when Kenneth joined them. All three men drank a final cup of coffee, before Kenneth said, 'I have my driver and car outside. It will take us the rest of the day to drive to the border with Idaho and the militia camp.'

Grinning, Jamison said, 'Let's go; we're burning daylight.'

Kenneth Turner with Lucian and Jamison sat in the mammoth new 1915 Buick Touring car in the back with the driver in front. The challenging ride, over roads both paved and unpaved, brought them to the militia camp in time for dinner.

The militia's camp, ten miles north of the Idaho border, was set on eight-hundred acres, with barracks for all the men, a mess hall, and quarters for the Turners and any guests. There were some two-hundred-fifty militia soldiers in training, broken down to twenty-man platoons.

A parade ground, exercise areas, shooting range, classrooms, latrines, communal showers, and lecture hall rounded out the camp. Lucian and Jamison met Kenneth's father Horatio Turner and Kenneth's son, Donnie, who was nine going on ten. The Turners and Hayes all ate in the mess hall with the militia.

After dinner, Horatio gave a long-winded speech to all the men about what was happening in America. The people who were trying to sully the way of life in America for all decent white Americans. He went on, yelling out derogatory terms for Negros, Jews, and southern Europeans, immigrants, and the like. The diatribe went on for over an hour. The men yelled back about their similar beliefs.

Horatio, Kenneth, and Lucian all had a final nightcap in the Officer's Club before going to bed. Lucian and Jamison crawled under the covers after blowing out the candles. Each had a single bed which was nowhere as pleasant as the hotel in Virginia City.

The day's ride had been long and tiring for both father and son. Jamison rolled over to face his father's bed. 'Dad, this is the real America here. I heard some of this stuff when we were at Camp Bliss and Benning, but this place is real. Do you think people like Turners will try to overthrow the government?'

'No, son, they can't. People like us in the Army won't let them. We might agree about how they feel toward some people but overthrow the government? Never. The Army would hunt them down, as we did with the Indians.'

Jamison asked, 'Do you think there are more militias out there?'

Lucian snorted. 'Yes, Jamie, there are many more piss-ants, rich white men who want to play at war but were too chickenshit to go into the Army.'

Jamison frowned. 'Dad, I know many people who don't cotton to aliens, Jews, and Negros.'

Lucian replied, 'I know there are, son, but this is America, and we already fought a Civil War to free the slaves, and we aren't going to fight another. We must uphold the Constitution and defend our country.'

Jamison thought about what his father said about duty and defense, but he didn't care about people who weren't like himself, no matter what others, or even his father, might say. Jamison was going to West Point and become an Army officer to save America from all foes against the country.

Lucian and Jamison spent the next ten days with the militia, watching the training methods, some in the art of being a soldier. Jamison had seen all the same things on military posts with his parents.

Lucian returned to the Presidio in Monterey, and Jamison went to West Point. Once home, Lucian went to his office, he wrote down all the events he experienced meeting Kenneth and Horatio Turner, the militia, and the KKK. As well as the Klan propaganda exposed at the camp.

Chapter 41

JB and Margarita were awake in the small house the waitress lived in. The waitress and the boy had left for work just before noontime. The bungalow was quiet in the rising heat outside. The street looked deserted. Mojave was a quiet little town with nowhere to go, and no one interested in getting there.

He wanted to get back to killing. The last person to fall under his knife had been found a couple of weeks earlier. The itch inside the man, that place he never could identify, needed to get scratched. It was like the people in Pamplona, Spain, from a newsreel at a movie house he had seen a few years ago. The people were running for their lives from the bulls. Just like he was running from the beast inside his soul.

They had two choices: take Rte. 14 north to Inyo County, or head south to Lancaster. JB knew that Lancaster was more significant than any town north and big enough to let him hide in plain sight. He could find some unsuspecting person, satisfy the beast with a kill, and dump the body in the surrounding desert.

JB found a motel for the night. After their nightly romp, Margarita fell into a deep sleep. He rose from the bed as she lay entwined in the sheet. He placed a *Do Not Disturb* sign on the doorknob and left her softly snoring.

He drove around until he found a deserted piece of highway. It was the shank of the evening, still early enough for him to see what he was after, but quiet time, with few cars on the road. He saw an older man in ragged clothes, dirty, with at least a week-old beard. The vagrant had a sack over his shoulder, presumably holding all his worldly possessions.

JB stopped. The vagrant stepped on the running board, held the door open, and then jumped onto the seat. Neither said a word. JB drove out from the center of town. The vagrant assumed that the driver wanted sex and that payment would follow. He had been through this routine many times before; for him, it was money in his pocket, not a lifestyle. The truck stopped a couple of hundred yards from the road, facing the open desert. It would be an easy kill.

JB hid the knife in his left hand. The vagrant turned toward him and reached for his belt. That was the moment JB thrust this knife into the man's abdomen, twisted the blade, and pulled it upward. Clean and straightforward. The vagrant's mouth formed an O as his life quietly slipped away.

Going through the vagrant's pockets, JB found only a few dollars and a pocket knife. Taking the money, he thought about keeping the blade, but in the end, he left it with the stranger. He reached over the body, opened the door, and pushed the man out onto the desert.

The beast was satisfied at last. Life was good when you were in charge.

A Los Angeles County sheriff's deputy found the body when he saw vultures flying overhead a few days later. The medical examiner in Los Angeles chalked this death up to 'the truck murderer.' The numbers were rising, but the official total was unknown. All local police and county sheriff's departments were out and ready for any sighting of the Dodge truck. Every officer wanted to be the one to bring down this killer who had passed over the roads and byways of Southern California.

Chapter 42

The day after the fiasco in Palm Springs, I was back at my office.

The FBI had agents working with locals in Arizona, near Kingman, and in all the counties of Southern California, looking for the missing Major Hayes, First Sergeant Arnold, and Scott Huddelson. He could also be known as Mort Beach.

Every structure belonging to a Hayes was being searched using Federal, State, and local law enforcement. The FBI was working with the authorities in Costa Rica at Hayes's vast ranch holdings there. The National Federal Police in Mexico searched all four holding Major Hayes has in southern Mexico. No Major Hayes, and all four properties were sold two months ago to local interests.

I sent a few deputies out to Keeler, to search the old zinc mining town and to Patrice Taggert's place in China Lake. Taggert is the last known living relative of Scott Huddelson. The frenzy was palpable in the office, but also among the officers. No one ever thought the elusive Major Jamison Hayes, First Sergeant Wade Arnold, or the possibly 'resurrected' Corporal Scott Huddelson could get through our dragnet.

The only unexpected call came from Dr. Crawley, the medical examiner of Los Angeles County and the itinerant ME for Inyo County.

Edith buzzed the intercom, 'Jim, I have Dr. Crawley on line two.'

'Thanks, Edith,' I pushed the button on my phone. 'Dr. Crawley, to what do I owe the pleasure of your call today?'

Dr. Crawley answered, 'Jim, my office completed the autopsy on a vagrant killed up in Lancaster. We ran prints on a knife found at the scene through the national database of the FBI in Washington.'

Surprised, I asked, 'When did the FBI get a national fingerprint database?'

Dr. Crawley laughed. 'It seems they created it in the 1920s. It's called the Identification Department, establishing a central repository of criminal identification data for US law enforcement agencies.' He took a breath and continued, 'Sorry, Jim. I just found out about it myself. I forgot that you probably haven't heard of it either. Right now, all the prints are being classified manually. I've been told they have an ever-growing staff trying to keep up with it.'

'Wow. So the FBI can cross-check murders from different states now.' I shook my head in amazement.

'Yeah, it's a wonder that they can do this, even if it does take weeks to find a match. The great thing is,' Dr. Crawley said excitedly, 'the wizards at the FBI came up with this: there is only one unknown offender, who is at the center of all the single random killings in Southern California, four other western states, and Mexico over the last twenty years. There is no match to a specific individual, but when the killer is caught and we match his prints, we have the killer.'

I sat horrified, hearing the news. 'Tell me about the killer.'

Over the next twenty minutes, Dr. Crawley informed me of all the deaths attributed to this individual. The information was appalling. How did one man kill all these innocent people and fade into the background unobserved? Not a sole witness, but various descriptions of a nondescript male between thirty and fifty initially seen in a 1940 Chevy truck and now possibly a 1943 Dodge truck. The only other news of the perpetrator was from the junkyard where the Chevy truck was found—the man was no longer alone. He might have a woman riding along with him.

Dr. Crawley went on, 'A call received by the task force assigned to find the murderer was a tip from a woman living alone in Running Springs, just south of Lake Arrowhead near Big Bear Lake in San Bernardino County. The woman told the tip line that between 1950 and 1958, a man—she never knew his name—would stop by her place for a drink of water. The man she described was someone she met at a bar in Big Bear; after a long night of drinking boilermakers, she took him to her home for four days.'

Shaking my head in wonder, I wrote everything down. 'Go on, Doctor.'

'This woman went on to say the man in the Chevy came around every two to six months, staying for a few days and then moving on. He never mentioned his name or told her what kind of work he did, and never said where he was going.' Dr. Crawley paused a moment, and I heard what sounded like a page being turned.

Finally, he continued, 'The woman ended her story by saying the visits stopped abruptly in 1958. She never saw or heard from him again. She figured he was killed by some husband or boyfriend who caught him messing with a woman.'

'That's an amazing story, Dr. Crawley. Any other information from the task force?'

Doctor Crawley went on, 'Another call came into the task force yesterday from another woman who lived outside of Kingman, Arizona. She told a similar story about the man in the Chevy stopping by. She said she had a son, who she named Toby, by him back in 1956. The man came by her place in January of this year. She said he stayed for about four hours on this last trip. He never told her his name or where he had been.'

'Wow, that's a lot of information to come in on him.'

'Yeah. But what I don't understand is this.' Dr. Crawley paused before adding, 'Both these women relayed that this man was kind and generous.'

'They're lucky to be alive.'

The unknown man reminded me of Silas Reid, the Hanging Murderer, who faded into the background in his day-to-day life. Silas never caused a fuss with others or the police. Were men like Silas always out there?

Dr. Crawley had more to say. 'Sheriff Cobb, the latest tip came in from a bar owner down in Thermal, about a young woman named Margarita who worked there and left the restaurant about seven or eight weeks ago. She left with a man driving an old Chevy truck.'

The last thing Dr. Crawley said to me was, 'The task force thinks the killer and this Margarita, no known last name, are headed north.'

I sat at my desk and contemplated the idea of setting up a roadblock on State Rte. 395, the only highway running south to north in Inyo County. I was a little short on deputies since sending a few of my people to Keeler, China Lake, and looking for Hayes, Arnold, and Huddelson.

The idea of getting the Chevy killer off the road was gnawing at my soul. Like an old war wound that signaled a change in the weather, I wanted to find this evil, serial killer bad, but the lack of personnel forced me to rely on the CHP to watch the highways.

I put a call into the CHP Office in Bishop. After getting them up to date on the killer's exploits over the last twenty-five years and that he was now driving a 1940s Dodge truck, the CHP was ready to track down the unknown killer and his female companion. I had a deep urge to bring in the mass killer alive, hear his story as to why he committed all those killings, and then send him off to San Quentin and the apple green room, where he would be strapped to a chair, waiting to breathe in the hydrocyanic gas.

This would be a fitting death for the man in the truck. But what about the young woman who might be with him? Did he abduct her? Is she still alive?

Chapter 43

I had just ended my conversation with the CHP in Bishop when Edith buzzed my intercom. 'Jim, Carl Magnus is on the line from Palm Springs.'

'Thanks, Edith, I'll pick up.'

I pushed the button for the line. 'Carl, what's going on down in Palm Springs?'

'Jim, it has gone to shit down here.'

'What happened?' I asked, confused.

'After searching the other two houses on the block, the local PD went to the cul-de-sac where General Lucian Hayes lived with his Asian helper. The general and his manservant were both found dead.'

'How? When...wait. What happened?' I asked, stunned.

Carl replied, 'They both received single gunshot wounds to the head. The general in his bed and the servant in the basement. It looked like the servant was trying to hide or escape.' Carl paused to catch his breath before he continued. 'No forced entry into the house and the ME down here placed their time of deaths around midnight.'

I sat back in my chair and groaned. 'Did the Palm Springs Police find anything else?'

Carl snorted. 'Yeah, all three residences had tunnels that connected each to the other. I figure that was how the mystery gardener got away yesterday.'

My intercom buzzed again. 'Hold on Carl, I have another call.' Before I could hear Magnus acknowledge my request, I switched calls.

'Jim, this is Red, down in China Lake, at Patrice Taggert's house. She's been murdered in her home. She's still warm, so it looks like whoever killed her left just before we arrived.'

'Damn it! Thanks, Red.' Before I hung up, I told Red, 'This may very well be the brother, Scott. Look around there for any hidden rooms or secret passages. Ask the neighbors if a guy around forty was seen in the area recently.'

'Okay, Jim, I'll get right on it.'

I hung up on Red and returned to Carl Magnus to relay the information about Patrice Taggert. My morning seemed like it was non-stop information overload. I was dizzy with the unsettling news.

Sitting at my desk didn't reveal any answers.

Did the same person or people who killed the general and his servant also kill Patrice Taggert?

Where were Hayes and Arnold? Was the gardener Mort Beach really Huddelson?

Noon was approaching; what was next?

Chapter 44

I had arrived for lunch, but it seemed like it was the Fourth of July, Christmas, my birthday, and my anniversary wrapped all in one. My house was full, with a party atmosphere. Conchita and the children were sitting at the table with Merrill and Delfina, in front of a giant cake. Conchita's sister Rosita and her family were also around the table. I walked in to find everyone laughing and having fun, while I was neck-deep in unsolved murders and a criminal on the loose, possibly in my own county.

I went into the kitchen, and Conchita came to me and gave me a big kiss as our three children welcomed me home.

Conchita said, 'Jim, we are so glad you came home for lunch. We are having a party today. Merrill has something to tell you.'

I looked at my father, who was laughing and hanging on to Delfina. I said, 'Dad, let me in on the fun. I could use a little of that right about now.'

'Jim, I asked Delfina to marry me. She said yes, and we plan to split our time—six months here and the other six in Zihuatanejo.'

'That sounds great. When is the wedding?' I asked.

'We plan to tie the knot this Sunday here at the ranch. Family, a few old friends; nothing extravagant. Is that okay with you, son?'

'Wow,' I looked around and back at Merrill. 'Dad, of course, it's okay with me. I'm… we're all happy for you and Delfina, congratulations.'

The news rocked my world. I should have expected my father would want to marry his companion of several years. I thought if they were happy and out of my hair, what else could I ask for in life? I knew that Conchita would fill me in later tonight. Life was good, for the moment.

I ate my lunch of chicken *mole*, luxuriated in the various tastes, and enjoyed a cake in celebration of the upcoming nuptials. My only wish was that Marlene would be out of town this coming weekend.

The celebration at home caused me to get back to the office late; it was pushing at two o'clock when I arrived. Edith was fixing her makeup as I walked past her. She looked like she'd had a rendezvous with Alex Morgan.

I walked in my office thinking; *I hope Edith has found a keeper this time; she deserves it for once.*

Before I sat down, Edith buzzed me. 'Jim, Red is on the phone.'

I picked up. 'Red, what have you learned?'

'I talked with Carl Magnus down in Palm Springs. The weapon used in those murders may be the same one used on Patrice Taggert. We also found a secret basement room in Taggert's house. It looks like a man was living down there off and on.'

'Red,' I surmised, 'I bet... well, maybe that man could be our once-dead Corporal Huddelson. The brother Patrice Taggert knew nothing about.'

'I think you're on to something, Jim,' Red said.

'How so, Red?'

'There are all kinds of mementos from the 4th Infantry Division, the battles the unit was involved in. There also is a picture of Huddelson's grave in France.'

'Red, we have an APB out on Hayes, Arnold, and Huddelson. Let them know he might be using the alias Mort Beach. Maybe others. Did you hear anything about Hayes or Arnold?'

'Among the things we found down in the basement room, there was an article about the war-injured Major Hayes living in Indian Wells after the armistice in 1945. His left arm was amputated; he suffered the injury in a car accident outside of Paris on August 15, 1944.'

'Well, Red, I guess our missing Major Hayes did sustain a war injury after all.'

'The newspaper article, from the *L.A. Post*, plays down any war reference. The article talks about the unceremonious return of the major in December 1944. No parade, medals, or fanfare.' Red paused a moment. 'The major's wife died from complications of surgery in May 1940. They had no children.'

'Red, I want you to get someone to run down all the information about the late Mrs. Hayes; the how, when, where, and why. It may help us understand the missing Major Hayes.'

It seems that once a question is answered, another one is asked. How far down the rabbit hole were we all going to go?

Chapter 45

The pharmacy in Lone Pine was still open for a final customer at five minutes after six p.m.

'Here's your prescription, Mrs. Fuller; thanks for waiting.' Owen Snyder handed over the bag containing the medicine.

'I'm happy that you could get my husband's prescriptions ready, even though it's after hours. Good night, Owen.'

'Good evening, Mrs. Fuller; give my best to Richard.'

Owen was ready to close up shop for the night and head home to his wife and children. Before he could turn around, the three bells above the front door rang, signaling a new customer.

Owen called out, 'I'm sorry, but I'm getting ready to close the store.'

The man shut and locked the door, turning over the *Closed* sign. He was wearing a long duster coat made from oilcloth, and a black Stetson hat pushed down over his eyes, leaving his face shadowed. The man's spurs jangled on the back of his dusty boots as he walked down an aisle to the rear of the store. He looked more than six feet tall, with a muscular upper body. He stood in front of the raised partition. Owen was behind it.

Owen looked at the man. 'I'm sorry, sir, but the store is closed.'

'Tonight, I think you will stay open, Mr. Snyder.' The man's voice was haunting, so low that Owen needed to lean over the counter to understand the stranger.

'Okay, what can I do for...'

Before Owen could finish his question, the man grabbed Owen by his collar and pulled him over the counter, his leg brace scraping the countertop, throwing him onto the floor. Putting his left knee on Owen's chest, the man quickly punched Owen three times in the face.

The crunch of facial bones with each punch. A three-inch laceration above his left eye was half an inch wide, bleeding, forcing Owen's eyelid closed. Owen couldn't defend himself, even if he had the strength. He wanted to cry out for mercy, but no words came.

The stranger sensed that Owen was ready to pass out. He pulled Owen up by his coat lapels and said, 'Don't ever talk to the sheriff again about your brother, or the same will happen to you. I'll kill you and your entire fucking family, just like I did your brother.' The man dropped Owen to the floor. He stood up, kicking Owen in the gut and his chest before turning around, and he stomped out of the store.

Owen's right eye was open but blurred. He kept his head still on the floor and tried to keep breathing. He was afraid the nightmares Wally had for twenty years were just starting for him.

A short time later, the phone rang in the back office of the pharmacy; Owen knew his wife Emily was calling, worried that he hadn't arrived home. The ringing stopped.

Owen slipped into unconsciousness, wanting all the hurt to go away.

A half-hour later, Emily rushed through the front door of the store and ran to her husband. She cradled his head in her arms. 'Owen, what happened? Who did this to you?'

Barely able to speak, he was going in and out consciousness. he whispered, 'Emily, I don't know…it was a stranger. The man said he killed Wally.' Owen sobbed, spitting blood. 'And, and he would kill you and the children if I didn't do what he wanted.'

Crying, Emily asked, 'Owen, what can we do? Where can we go?'

Trying to comfort his wife, Owen hugged her arm. 'Emily, go to the office and phone for the ambulance and Sheriff Cobb.'

Emily ran to the office as darkness came over Owen.

Chapter

46

I walked into the hospital a few minutes after eight p.m. Red was waiting for me in the lobby. I asked, 'What do we know?'

Red frowned. 'Owen Snyder was in his pharmacy, alone, when a stranger came in and beat the shit out of him.'

'Damn.' I rubbed my eyes. 'Where is he now?'

'The emergency room with Dr. Daniels; he's new in town since the first of the year.'

We walked to the emergency room bed that had a drape pulled around it. I cleared my throat to get some attention. The curtain pulled back, and the doctor walked over.

I said, 'Hello, I'm Sheriff Cobb, and this is Deputy Sheriff Fowler.'

'I'm Doctor Daniels,' He replied as we all shook hands.

'How's Owen?'

'He has suffered a concussion and a fracture of all his left orbital bones. Three ribs are also broken. He was in and out of consciousness.' Dr. Daniels paused, 'He is being sent to UCLA Medical Center for surgery.'

The brutality of the attack shocked me. 'Can I speak with Owen before he leaves?'

'Yes, of course; his wife is with him now,' the doctor replied.

Red and I walked over to the bed. Owen had a large bandage covering the left side of his face. Emily was holding his left hand, and tear tracks stained her cheeks.

Softly, I said, 'Owen, it's Jim Cobb, can you tell me what happened?'

Owen spoke slowly. 'Jim, I'm glad that you came before...' he took a shaky breath. 'It was a stranger, Jim; I never saw him before. A big man, over six feet with a big chest and strong arms and hands.' I could see Owen's grip on his wife's hand tighten as he spoke. 'He was wearing a black Stetson and a duster overcoat, like a cowboy. He came in just after Bonnie Fuller left with her prescription.'

'I'm sorry this happened to you, Owen,' I ran my hand over my head and sighed. 'Did he say anything?'

'I told him the store was closed. He came up to the counter, pulled me over the countertop, and threw me on the floor.' Owen started to tremble as he spoke. 'He punched me in the face three times, then crouched down and said in a menacing voice that I was not to talk to you about Wally. He said he had killed my brother.' Tears started to run down his cheek.

'It's okay, Owen, you're safe now. Take it, easy buddy.' I waited for Owen to calm a bit before asking, 'Is there anything else you can tell us about the man? Distinguishing features, scars, tattoos, anything at all?'

Red asked, 'Was he white or Mexican?'

Owen replied, 'He was Caucasian. He punched me so hard I thought I was going to die. I passed out after he left.'

I nodded. 'Anything else you can remember?'

Owen turned his head slightly back and forth before a light went on inside his brain. 'Yes, Jim, he came into the store, locked the door, and turned the closed sign around. He smelled of smoke on his clothes and breath.' Owen sank back into the bed, drained from relaying the information.

Emily looked as though her entire life had passed before her eyes as her husband struggled to speak. 'Sheriff, this stranger almost killed my husband. He threatened to kill Owen, me, and our children.'

'I understand, Emily. The sheriff's department will stop at nothing to find this man, and we will keep you all safe.'

I looked at Owen Snyder, an educated man living a life of pain due to polio, his brother murdered, and his parent's dead some fifteen years now. I had no right to ask anything else from my friend.

'Thanks, Owen, you've been a great help, Red and I will leave you to rest before you go down to UCLA.'

As Red and I walked out of the room, I said, 'Red, get the *Closed* sign from the pharmacy, get it dusted for prints, and send a guard to UCLA with Owen and Emily. Find out where the kids are staying and get a guard there, too. I want him guarded day and night. I'm going to see Bonnie and Richard Fuller.'

On the way out, I ran into Dr. Daniels. 'I understand you are new to our town. Glad to have new blood at the hospital.'

'Yes, and my wife is an anesthesiologist here at the hospital.'

'That is fantastic. Where did you come from?'

'We were born and raised in Chicago. My parents came with us. They want the high desert clear air, and a smaller community. And we have two children, a boy and a girl.'

'This is a great place to raise kids. A lot of good people here.'

And some very bad ones, I thought.

Chapter 47

I drove over to Bonnie and Richard Fuller's house in Lone Pine. It was a two-story Victorian built back in the 1920s. The couple had raised three children, a son and two daughters. All the children had since been to college and left Inyo County for more lucrative areas of the state and started families.

I knocked on the front door. Bonnie answered, only opening the door halfway. 'Good evening, Sheriff Cobb. What brings you out on a night like tonight?'

It had started to rain when I was in the hospital.

I held my hat in my hands. My face wet from the rain. 'Hello Bonnie, I've just come from the hospital. I was looking in on Owen Snyder from the pharmacy. Owen was beaten up in his store, minutes after you left. I need to talk with you about what you remember.'

'Oh, God! Come in, Sheriff. Is Owen okay? What happened?' She opened the door entirely and directed me to what was the parlor when the house was built.

Bonnie was in her sixties, with a pixie cut short blond hair, a smiling, happy face, blue eyes, and a can-do attitude. She worked with several volunteer groups in the county. She was a mover and shaker in town, organizing potluck dinners, fundraisers for good causes, and working on stage plays put on at the Valley Workshop.

I took off my rain slicker and put it over a chair in the kitchen and my wet hat hanging off the back rail.

'Please, Jim, have a seat on the divan and tell me what happened to Mr. Snyder.'

Richard Fuller was sitting in a leather wingback chair. Richard, a good ten years older than his wife, had sold farm machinery for a living and had retired twelve years ago. He was thin, with a wiry build, thinning grayish-brown hair, and gray eyes. In his retirement, he played golf up and down the eastern slope of the state. He loved to play a new poker game with local friends called Texas Hold'em, or just Hold'em.'

'Good evening, Richard,' I shook his hand before sitting down.

Richard said, 'The rain is really coming down.'

I told the Fullers about the assault on Owen Snyder inside the store.

'Bonnie, Owen said that you picked up a prescription right at closing time. When you left the store, did you see a man outside?'

'Why yes, Sheriff, I bumped right into him. I'd never seen him before, but he was tall. He was wearing a black Stetson and a duster coat.' She frowned a moment, thinking. 'I couldn't see his face since his hat was down low over his eyes. I don't think he was clean-shaven.'

I asked, 'Did the man say anything?'

Bonnie shook her head. 'No. I apologized for walking into him, but he just grunted and walked around me before entering the store.'

I wrote down everything she told me. 'If I showed you a group of pictures of a few suspects, could you recognize him?'

'I don't know, but I can give it a try,' she replied.

'Can you come to the office tomorrow morning at around ten? It won't take long.'

'Okay, I'll come down tomorrow.' She looked down, then up at me. 'I'll do anything I can.'

Nodding, I asked, 'Is there anything else you remember about the man?'

'Yes, there was, Sheriff. His clothing smelled of smoke, like from a fire, his upper body was big, hard, and intimidating, and his hands were rough, like he worked outdoors.'

'Thanks, Bonnie, if you think of anything else tell, me tomorrow. That will be all for now. I've taken up enough of your time, I'd best be getting home myself.'

Richard shook my hand again, 'Thanks for coming by Sheriff.'

'I'll call Red and get a patrol car and a couple of deputies to stay out front.'

###

I returned to the office and found Red still there. 'Bonnie Fuller will be by at ten a.m. tomorrow. Get some pictures together—Wade Arnold, Scott Huddelson, and Jamison Hayes. I'm betting that Huddelson is our attacker.'

Red frowned. 'We have an APB out on all three men, no sightings.'

'Send a patrol car and deputies over to the Fuller house. I want them watched in case this guy comes back to harm Bonnie.'

'I'm on it, Jim,' Red said.

Looking at my messages, I asked, 'Did the deputies check all the properties that Hayes owns, and any other places Huddelson might be hiding out?'

Red replied, 'Yes, Jim, I've got everyone working their asses off.'

I stood and looked at Red. 'I want the man who did this to Owen found, and then I want a few minutes alone with him. No one comes into my county, where I live and does this to my friend.'

Red nodded and didn't say another word. He went to his office and started calling for other deputies.

I sat at my desk, thinking about what kind of man kills a man like Wally and then goes and beats up his brother. The world was getting darker with each day, evil was always around, and I wanted to protect my family, friends, and the people I served.

Chapter 48

Lancaster, California, is seventy miles northeast of downtown Los Angeles, but still inside the county limits. The summer heat regularly hits triple digits. The census of 1960 counted a population of roughly Twenty Six Thousand, with the largest group of people living inside the city limits being Mexican. It was the perfect location for the scraggly-looking JB, driving a beat-up 1943 Dodge truck, and the sultry twenty-something Margarita.

The couple had been together for about four months and were currently staying in the same one-bedroom, one-story ranch stucco duplex they had moved into after leaving the little town of Mojave.

Three weeks after settling into the duplex, JB started to feel that old itch beginning. He was antsy, sweaty, and annoyed. He needed a release, but he knew that satisfying the urge in Lancaster was not possible. He needed another place to find his prey.

Margarita finished washing the dishes. She wiped her hands with a dishcloth before sitting down on the plaid couch in the living room. She pulled JB's legs onto her lap, then began to rub his feet.

Margarita looked over at JB. 'Hey, *cabrón*, I know that you are all jumpy and out of sorts living in this dump. I think you need to go out on your own and find what you need to settle yourself down. I don't want you to take it out on me. I'm not a punching bag. Go do what you do and come back to me; I'll be here ready to fuck your eyeballs out.'

JB glared at her. '*Chica*, you think you know what I need?'

She laughed, '*Cabrón*, you are easier to read than the funny papers.'

He sat up and grabbed her chin. 'I could beat the shit out of you.'

Margarita smiled. 'If you do, in the morning, you will find your chest with a big knife sticking out of it.'

'*Lo entiendo, Chica.*' He put on his socks and boots and pushed himself off the couch, walking out the front door.

'Bring home some vanilla ice cream, *el jefe,*' she called after him.

Margarita was sleeping on the couch alone at three a.m. She woke, thinking the fool came home and didn't wake her. Margarita looked in the bedroom, nothing. Then she checked out the freezer compartment of the fridge, looking for vanilla ice cream. Empty. Maybe the fool got in a fight and was dead, or in jail. *Time will tell,* she thought. She went to the bed and fell instantly asleep.

Whatever JB needed to make himself right was all on his dime, it had nothing to do with Margarita. Yes, she wanted him safe and able to care for her when he came back, but if he never returned, she would remember what he did to wake up her inner self and chase the fear of loneliness away.

Chapter 49

Red showed Owen pictures of Wade Arnold, Scott Huddelson, and Jamison Hayes a couple of days after his surgery. Owen picked Scott Huddelson as his assailant. Owen returned home after a week and a half in the hospital and started back at work.

I instructed Red to have round the clock protection for Owen and his family.

The APBs out on Wade Arnold, Scott Huddelson, and Jamison Hayes hadn't given the department any leads.

Frustration concerning the case was making me edgy, and tomorrow will also be a little tense—my dad and Delfina Ruiz will be married at the house. The dark cloud over the entire affair was Marlene Chambers.

I made sure that all the guests from the sheriff's department swore not to say a word to Marlene. This marriage and party needed to stay on the QT. I've been silently praying to God to keep an eye out for her and let this celebration come off without a hitch.

I was home in time for dinner, Conchita, made pork tamales, with both red and green sauces. The kids and I dug into the feast with reckless abandon, acting like this was our last meal. Since I didn't know what tomorrow would bring, I wanted to make my last meal fill me up. My plate empty, no leftovers insight, I sat in my chair at the head of the table, rubbing my expanded abdomen with the added joy, if I died in my sleep, I at least had the last meal to end all lasts meals. Content, sated, and overfull, I was lost for words.

Conchita, sat in the chair next to mine, 'Do you have a plan if Marlene shows up tomorrow?'

I looked at my wife's beautiful face and realized I didn't have a plan B. In my mind, a dark cloud covered my head with a hurricane storm raining down on me, unable to answer Conchita's question.

###

The day was gorgeous, a cloudless sapphire blue sky with only a little breeze, and the temperature in the eighties. My father was beaming in a new Western shirt and string tie. He had asked me to be his best man, which I happily accepted. The reverend was from the Episcopal church in town, the same church Mom and Dad were married in, back in 1911.

Red escorted Delfina down the hall to our large family room. They walked to where the reverend was standing, as the Wedding March played on our record player. Red lifted the lace veil, kissed Delfina on the cheek, and gave her hand to Merrill. Conchita stood next to the bride as the matron of honor.

I breathed a small sigh of relief, thinking this affair was going to go off without a hitch.

As the reverend began to speak, the front door to our house was kicked open, and there stood Marlene Chambers holding a 12-gauge pump-action shotgun from the armory at the sheriff's department. It seemed to be a precise moment the world stood still, the air was sucked out of the house, and we were all standing in some sort of suspended, alternate universe.

Marlene cried out, 'No Mexican whore is going to marry Merrill Cobb unless it is over my dead body!' She pulled the trigger, blew a shot through the ceiling, and racked another round in place.

Everyone in the room stared at Marlene with their mouths open, waiting for the next shoe to fall. Everyone but Delfina.

Delfina walked to the back of the room and stood toe-to-toe with Marlene.

Delfina asked, 'You and what fucking army are going to stop this wedding, *gringa*?'

Marlene was speechless. She had the first part of her drama thought out—barge in the house, halt the wedding, and fire the shotgun; end of the event. The idea of someone confronting her never occurred to Marlene. She let the barrel of the shotgun point directly at Delfina.

Conchita grabbed the kids and rushed into the bedroom.

'I'm stopping this farce of a wedding. No Mexican whore is coming between Merrill and me.'

Delfina looked straight into Marlene's eyes, and before Marlene knew what was happening, Delfina took the barrel in her left-hand, lifting in straight up and punched Marlene with a roundhouse right. The shotgun fell out of Marlene's hands. She dropped to the floor, like a steer at a slaughterhouse after being shot in its head.

I saw Edith Pearson and Alex Morgan standing at the back of the invited guests, 'Edith, call for an ambulance.'

Tom and Gabe were hiding behind their mother, and my little Rosie yelled, 'One punch knockout!'

The rest of the guests stood around, looking aghast, not knowing what to say or do. No one needed to fear, Delfina knew what she did and how to go on.

Delfina looked at the laughable excuse for an adversary lying on the floor, then opened her right hand to look at the roll of nickels she held. She placed the turn in the hidden pocket of her wedding gown.

This little item had been in Delfina's possession since 1943 when she had to deal with another woman who stepped over the bounds of propriety involving another man. Everything secured, and the guests none the wiser.

Delfina turned and walked back to the alter. She flexed her hand to relieve any soreness, took Merrill's hand, and requested, 'Let's continue, Padre, please.'

Everyone laughed, relieved, and thankful no one had been shot.

The reverend said, 'Delfina and Merrill, I now pronounce you husband and wife. Merrill, you can kiss the bride.'

The ceremony over, the groom kissed his bride, and the party commenced.

Conchita took my hand and whispered in my ear, 'What are you going to do about Marlene?'

Shrugging, I said, 'For now, nothing.'

Edith held Marlene's head in her lap on the floor, waiting for medical help.

Two deputies came out to the house, along with the ambulance attendees who picked up the unconscious Marlene, placed her in the back of the ambulance, and drove her to the hospital. I told the deputies, 'After the hospital, put Marlene in a cell at the jail.'

The party continued into the wee hours of the morning. No one talked about the interruption by the most hateful person who ever worked in the department. They were too busy celebrating with Merrill and Delfina.

After everyone finally left, and we got the kids settled in bed, Conchita and I walked hand in hand to our bedroom.

I kissed her before saying, 'It's time for Marlene to retire. If Delfina ever sees her again, I don't think Marlene will survive.'

'What about Merrill?' she asked.

I smiled. 'I hope Merrill stays in line, or we'll be attending his funeral.'

Conchita laughed like a young girl getting a prize, giggly, infectious, and without a doubt, the best part of my day.

I shook my head. 'What about our daughter?'

'Jim, Rosie is the next announcer at a fight.'

We both laughed.

Chapter 50

My father and my new stepmother were off to Santa Barbara for a week-long honeymoon on the tranquil beach. My office was quiet for a Monday morning, then Carl Magnus and Sam Ludo walked in, just as my phone rang.

'Yes, this is Sheriff Cobb, what can I do for you?'

'This is Captain Craig Radcliffe of the San Diego PD, down here in San Ysidro. I have someone here that you sent out an APB on, a man by the name of Scott Huddelson.'

I was taken aback with the news. I shook my head. 'Captain, this is Sheriff Jim Cobb in Inyo County. Did you say that you apprehended Scott Huddelson?'

'Yes, Sheriff, Mr. Huddelson is sitting in one of our exam rooms.'

'This is fantastic news! My office has been searching for the suspect for quite a while. I will have my office arrange for transfer. First, Captain, was anyone else with Huddelson?'

'No, he was alone, trying to cross the border.'

'Thank you. Let me get on it from this end.'

I punched in the intercom. 'Edith, put Red on the line to get transfers of Scott Huddelson from San Ysidro.'

A few minutes later Red came in my office, 'Transfer set up, I have a car and two officers going south. They should get back here late tonight.'

Red and I are both smiling.

'Thanks Red, now all we need to know is where Jamison Hayes and Wade Arnold are.'

###

By two the next morning, Scott Huddelson was in our custody. At seven a.m., Carl Magnus, Sam Ludo, and I entered the interrogation room. The room was eight by ten feet and windowless, furnished with only a metal table and four metal chairs. A one-way mirror was mounted on the wall facing the accused. Red watched from a small room on the other side.

Huddelson wore a striped prisoner shirt and pants over his six-foot stature, and a wan face. Looking straight ahead, he was stiff and defiant.

Carl asked the first question, 'Scott, please tell us about yourself; where you were born, family, et cetera.'

'My name is Corporal Scott Huddelson, U.S. Army, serial number 19 820 954.'

We looked at each other, dumbfounded. I said, 'Scott, tell us where you are from.'

'My name is Corporal Scott Huddelson, U.S. Army, serial number 19 820 954.'

Sam Ludo took a shot at it. 'Son, I'm in the Army; Army CID Agent Captain Sam Ludo. Now, please answer the question. Where are you from?'

'Sir, the Geneva Convention states that I only have to give you my name, rank, and serial number. My name is Corporal Scott Huddelson, U.S. Army, serial number 19 820 954. I consider myself a prisoner of war, a war that I have been engaged in since joining the California National Guard under Major Jamison Hayes in April 1941.'

We looked at each other, not really knowing what to do next. I got up from my chair, left the interrogation room, and went into the small room next door. 'Red, take Mr. Huddelson back to his cell.'

'Okay, Jim, what do we do next?'

I looked at Red and shrugged. 'I wish I knew. I've never interrogated a member of our own military when he thought he was an enemy combatant.'

Magnus and Ludo joined Red and me while Huddelson continued to sit ramrod straight in the interview chair.

'Gentlemen, I think we need to get a psychiatrist in here to talk to this fruitcake,' Ludo said.

I said, 'We need to find either Wade Arnold or Jamison Hayes to get some answers.'

The various agencies had come up empty as to the whereabouts of Hayes and Arnold. The two missing persons had vanished into thin air.

The situation with Huddelson remained. How to get him to talk?

And why did he kill his sister, Patrice Taggert?

Chapter 51

Two weeks after arresting Scott Huddelson, we were no closer to getting the man to talk to the authorities. The FBI and the Army each brought in psychiatrists to find out why Huddelson wouldn't speak. They even tried to hypnotize him without any success. He insisted that he was a prisoner of war, and he only responded to questions with his name, rank, and serial number.

There were no leads on Jamison Hayes and Wade Arnold. The FBI, Army CID, and my own deputies searched every likely property in California. The CHP looked along every highway and byway to find a vehicle containing Hayes and Arnold, along with looking for the 1943 Dodge truck the suspected mass murder was driving. The FBI even went to Costa Rica, to check the houses there owned by Hayes. Neither man had a living relative of record. The FBI asked the National Police in Mexico to investigate the Hayes properties in southern Mexico and found all four sites were sold three months earlier.

A news conference was conducted outside FBI headquarters in Los Angeles, asking the public for any assistance in locating Jamison Hayes and Wade Arnold. A $10,000 reward was offered for the whereabouts of either man. The call line was immediately inundated with bogus calls and psychics, providing their skills in exchange for a fee. Fortunately, my office wasn't saddled with running down the leads from the calls made to the FBI.

The disgraced Marlene had been taken to Los Angeles, where an oral surgeon had wired her jaw together for eight weeks. She was sucking her food through a straw when I visited her to request that she find another town to live in. She asked for a letter of recommendation, to locate a job in another area. My offer was to drop all the charges against Marlene if she relocated.

Marlene decided the best decision was to relocate and not go to jail in Inyo County.

She was in the hospital for a week. Two weeks after being released, she left Inyo County, the day before the newly married Mr. and Mrs. Merrill Cobb returned from their honeymoon in Santa Barbara. There wasn't a going away party for Marlene, just a heartfelt sigh of relief as she drove away with all her earthly belongings in an enclosed trailer behind her car. The real estate broker put Marlene's house up for sale, and the proceeds would be put in an escrow account at the bank, which Marlene could use for buying another home in the future.

Merrill and Delfina stayed for another five days before returning to Zihuatanejo. Our children didn't want their grandparents to leave, but after Grandpa and *Abuela* promised to return soon; only then were the newlyweds able to get out of town.

I was pleased by the amount of love my children showed to their grandparents, and immensely proud.

That night, Conchita told me the story about Delfina's roll of nickels. We laughed and promised never to reveal the information. Knowing that Delfina had used rolled nickels in a paper sleeve as brass knuckles to stop Marlene cold amazed me. What was more intriguing was Delfina's foresight to bring them with her to the wedding.

Just before eleven a.m. on May 3rd, a call came in from the CHP Inland Communication Center in San Bernardino, the central office for all the counties east of L.A. and San Diego.

'Sherriff Cobb, this is Sergeant Eckley, down in San Bernardino, at the dispatch center. I'm calling about the murderer who has been driving around Southern California, Nevada, and Arizona over the last twenty years.'

'Yes, I received notification that this man recently started driving a 1943 Dodge truck, and the last notice said he has a young Mexican woman companion,' I replied.

'That is the man I'm calling about. A month ago, he killed a prostitute in Bakersfield, and two nights ago, he killed a young woman in Indio, California. In both cases, he left fingerprints identifying the murderer as the same man from all the previous murders.'

'Any leads as to his whereabouts?' I asked.

'We believe this killer does not live in or around the area of these last two murders. He drives to a location, scouts out a victim, kills her, or him, then leaves.' Eckley paused a moment. 'CHP thinks he may live in eastern L.A. County, San Bernardino, or Inyo County. Could be in a high desert area, or a congested area, hiding his truck in a garage.'

'Wow,' I said, 'That's a large area to cover. Do you have any news about the accomplice? Where or if the man works?'

Eckley agreed. 'Yeah, it's a large area, and there is nothing new about the woman we think he is still with; we don't think she is present at the murders. The only forensic evidence is from the suspect. There is no consensus about how the suspect makes his living.'

I leaned back in my chair, rubbing my eyes. 'Is this killer still driving the Dodge truck?'

'The truck is a mystery. There's no sighting of a vehicle matching the description during daylight hours. The women murdered were out alone, or after they finished working for the night. The local pimps have been interviewed and told to look out for the truck.'

Shaking my head, I said, 'You have certainly laid out a puzzling set of possibilities for this suspect, Sergeant Eckley. Do you have information as to his physical identity?'

Eckley said, 'The two women who came forward gave a description. Male Caucasian, forty-five to fifty years old, possibly five-feet-nine inches tall, medium built, no distinguishing features. He usually has a woman named Margarita with him, early twenties, five-feet-two, black hair, no distinguishing marks. The bartender in Thermal never knew her last name, but he did think she at one time was in the Sisters of Perpetual Mercy Orphanage. The orphanage denies any knowledge of this woman.'

I wrote down this new information. 'Do you have any likenesses of these two suspects?'

'I'm sending up one of our officers to deliver the police sketches. I'll call with more information as it comes in.'

I leaned forward and smiled. 'Thanks for all the news, I'll be here all day.'

'Sheriff Cobb, have a good day and good hunting.'

I started to think about the man driving the Dodge truck and his hiding the vehicle in a garage during the day.

What if I applied the daytime concealment ruse to Jamison Hayes and Wade Arnold? They could live in a house under someone else's name, in the area they know best and have a market deliver groceries to the home. I tabled that idea for the moment.

I thought about the Sisters of Perpetual Mercy Orphanage in Thermal. A visit to the orphanage looked like a likely place to start.

Chapter 52

I picked up my phone. 'Edith, ask Red to come to my office. Also, do you know where Carl Magnus and Sam Ludo are? If they are here, ask them to come in, too.'

'Magnus, and Ludo are down at Ft. Irwin. I'll send Red in pronto.'

A few minutes later, Red came into my office and sat. 'Red, I was on the phone with Sargent Eckley with the CHP down in San Bernardino, about this killer who's been driving around in a truck murdering men and women over the last twenty years. He likes to find victims late at night, leaving their bodies along the side of the road. The CHP thinks this murderer doesn't live where he kills, maybe residing east of the Grapevine in Eastern L.A. County, San Bernardino County, or here. Only coming out at night and maybe hiding his truck in a garage.'

Red nodded, impressed. 'That's a good idea he had, Jim, but what does he live on? What does he do for cash?'

'He has a companion, a young Mexican woman, first name Margarita, she may have lived at the Sisters of Perpetual Mercy Orphanage in Thermal.' I looked at Red to see if he was following my thoughts. 'Margarita was working at a bar in Thermal. A guy came in fitting the description of the *truck killer*, and she left the next day, no parting words to the barkeep.'

Red snorted while writing down this new information. I knew he was with me.

I took a deep breath. 'This Margarita could be working at another bar at night if our suspect is hiding out during the day.'

Red shook his head. 'What's your plan to find these two?'

'First, send deputies out to all the bars and restaurants in the county and see if they have a new woman working, a Mexican woman. Then call Sergeant Eckley and see if he can have local law or CHP do the same in San Bernardino County and eastern

L.A. County, Lancaster, and Palmdale areas. We are getting likenesses of the two suspects from the CHP.'

Red sat back and asked, 'Anything else?'

'I want you to call up the Palm Springs recorder and ask
about any properties bought since 1945. I want to see if any of
these new owners knew Jamison Hayes or Wade Arnold. I'll also
contact Magnus and Ludo to do the same from their end. Also,
they can get the names of all the men who served with Hayes
and Arnold.'

Red was getting up before I could give him another job to do.

'Red, I'm going to see the Sisters of Perpetual Mercy Orphanage in Thermal.'

Red nodded and left my office, and I called Conchita, 'I'm
headed out the door on my way down to Thermal, I need to talk
with the Sisters of Perpetual Mercy Orphanage.'

Laughing, she asked, 'Do you want to adopt a child?'

'No, no adoption, we can make our own; I have more fun
trying.'

'That's a better answer, Jim. Now, why go to Thermal?' Conchita's curiosity was piqued.

I smiled, knowing I'd confused her. 'The accomplice of a
murderer who's killed more than fifteen men and women in the
last twenty years may have grown up in the orphanage.'

'I'll have dinner warm in the oven when you return.'

Chapter 53

Rancho Mirage in the Coachella Valley was located between Palm Springs and Indian Wells. Settlements in the area went back to the 1920s. The Thunderbird Guest Ranch opened in 1946. Next to the golf course was a gated community of nine large homes situated on several cul-de-sacs. Twenty-four-hour a day security only let in homeowners and their guests. No one else was permitted, not even the local police.

A twelve-thousand-square-foot Spanish Colonial Revival-style palace stood at the end of one such cul-de-sac, named Desert Sky Trail. The home was built in late 1945; the deed stated that Mr. Steven Yale owned the property and had lived there since the completion of the house.

Interestingly, no one ever saw Steven Yale or knew him; all legal inquiries concerning Mr. Yale and the property were handled by the law firm of Jackson and Market in Palm Springs. If anyone asked the lawyers at the company if they had ever met the client, they would have been unable to ever recall seeing Mr. Yale.

The drapes were always drawn, never an outside light turned on, all provisions and supplies delivered by a Mexican man named Armando Villalobos, who had worked for General Lucian Richmond Hayes from the general's retirement in 1920, until a few weeks ago, when the general died. Armando had spent his entire life working at the family date farm in Indian Wells. Now in his early sixties, a widower with six children; he lived in Thermal.

On this Tuesday, May 8th, Armando drove his flatbed truck to the back of the large house on Desert Sky Trail. The boxes of supplies were all brought into the home with the help of Mr. An (meaning peace) Lee, a Chinese man who was even older than Armando, and who had worked for the Hayes family since 1910.

Mr. Lee and Armando discussed the weather, work on the date farm, and the outlook for the Dodgers at the new stadium in Chavez Ravine. Both men hoped to get a weekend off to travel to see their team at Dodger Stadium. It wasn't until after the supplies were stored that Armando and Mr. Lee discussed their foremost thought—revenge.

Both men had worked for and loved General Hayes. In their eyes, the general was a god. The brutal murder of General Hayes pushed these lifelong friends to devise a plan of retribution.

They were two aging men, minorities in the grand scheme of things in California. They hid in the shadows, out of the limelight, away from prying eyes, and the people who murdered their friend, employer, and the nicest person either ever knew. Getting revenge, they needed to act like men a third of their age, fight with the fierceness of a tiger, and were willing to surrender their lives in the name of the general.

Chapter 54

I arrived in Thermal looking for the Sisters of Perpetual Mercy Orphanage. The building was nondescript, located two blocks from the main drag. The three-story building was at least a hundred years old, with no exterior hints of a religious order; the outside paint was peeling, the double entrance doors had a worn-in appearance. As bad as an orphanage seemed, this enterprise looked worse.

I left my Dodge Cruiser on the street and walked through the front door. The inside was shabby and smelled of mothballs and sweat. To the left of the entrance, a weary-looking nun, in what looked like her late sixties, wore a black habit. She stood at a reception desk, working on a newspaper crossword puzzle.

'What can I do for you, sir?' she asked.

'I'm Sheriff Jim Cobb of Inyo County; I'd like to talk to some-one about a child you had here a few years ago.'

'I think I could answer any question you might have, Sheriff. I'm Sister Kathy.'

'My information from the Riverside Sheriff's Department is that a young Mexican woman came here when she was fourteen or fifteen, she is now in her early twenties. Her name is Margar-ita, no last name.' I continued, 'She left the orphanage, finding work at a local bar, the El Caminante Bar, here in Thermal.'

'Sheriff, we get a lot of Mexican girls coming to the orphanage but this girl named Margarita never came through here during the time you suggest.'

I frowned. 'Do any of your charges ever leave to work at bars in the area?'

'No, never, Sheriff. All the girls here who don't get adopted and go out in the world to work are trained to work in offices, like secretaries or bookkeepers.'

I stared straight into her eyes and said, 'How come I don't completely believe this scenario?'

'It doesn't matter if you accept what I said or not, it's the truth. All our girls are decent, law-abiding women ready to face the world with their heads held high.'

Nodding, I looked around the room and back at her. 'Sister Kathy, is that your real name?'

Surprised, she replied, 'Yes, what do you mean?'

I shook my head. 'I say that you are a fraud, the sheriff told me that there isn't any religious order called the Sisters of Perpetual Mercy. You are not a nun, and this building is a center for prostitution in the Coachella Valley.'

Before the woman dressed as a nun could utter a word, three members of the Riverside sheriff's department entered through the back entrance. They handcuffed *Sister Kathy* and two accomplices, along with eight young women who worked as prostitutes.

All the women we arrested were placed in cells in the jail located next door to the sheriff's office in Thermal. The sheriff knew about the prostitution in the area but was never able to connect the Sisters of Perpetual Mercy Orphanage and the nuns to the illegal enterprise.

The woman who introduced herself as Sister Kathy to Jim Cobb was the madam, named Agnes Dempsey. She was seventy years old and had started in life during the First World War in San Diego. She moved on to become the madam of a place run by the local mafia in Los Angeles.

After a big raid in 1933, Agnes packed up all her belongings and moved out to the desert. She opened her establishment in 1934 and paid off enough locals to stay in business, but when there were no taxes paid on the property, the State Board of Licensing called up the Riverside sheriff.

Agnes Dempsey was placed in an interview room. Lieutenant Lyle Murphy of the sheriff's department and I sat across from her.

I leaned forward. 'Agnes, now that we know who you are and what you do, I again want to ask you about Margarita.'

Agnes sat back in her chair. 'Margarita was a steady worker, made herself and me a lot of money, then she met a man old enough to be her father. They clicked, and she said she was going to leave town with him. I never talked to her again.'

'What is Margarita's last name? What is her history?' I asked, pulling out my notepad.

'Margarita Gutiérrez. Her parents were migrants who came from Tecate, in Baja California, when she was six. She had an older brother who worked with the parents for the date farmers, then headed down to the Salton Sea for other produce. The brother brought Margarita to my place; he said she was fourteen. He told me his parents and another brother all died in a head-on crash. He was going to the central valley for work, and he couldn't take Margarita.

Lieutenant Murphy asked, 'At fourteen, did you force her into prostitution?'

Shaking her head, Agnes said, 'No, no, she wasn't ready, because she wasn't fourteen; maybe eleven or twelve. The two brothers, neither one looked older than sixteen, thought the cops might pick them up if Margarita was with them, and they would charge them as a pedophiles.'

'What did this young Margarita do?' I asked.

'I put her to work cleaning, washing, cooking, all-around chores. When she did get to the other side of fifteen, she had filled out and looked twenty-five. The girl was hungry to make some money.' Agnes smiled as she continued. 'She learned quick, I always had to watch out for her safety because I knew she was the one, the one to make me money. Then this fuck with a beat-up old Chevy truck came to town and took my honeypot away. I never found out his name, where he came from, or what he did for a living. When you find that fucker, kill him for me.'

'Didn't she live at this bar, El Caminante, or The Wayfarer Bar?'

'Yes, she did, Lieutenant, and every morning I went there to pick up what she owed me.'

Lieutenant Murphy asked, 'Agnes, my men found this picture in your office. Is this a picture of Margarita Gutiérrez?'

Agnes held the picture up to get a better look, 'This is Margarita right after she turned eighteen, but she still looked just like this when she left with the pig in the Chevy truck.'

Murphy and I left the interrogation room. I felt dirty after hearing what that excuse for a human being did to Margarita

Gutiérrez. I departed Thermal with a better identification picture of Margarita, and a last name, Gutiérrez.

'Put the photo of Margarita with the composite drawing of the unknown man driving the truck I received from the CHP, Sergeant Eckley.'

I needed to find the couple before he or they killed another innocent victim.

I understood the necessity for prostitutes in communities where working men couldn't meet and find eligible women to share their lives. Still, the madams of the world made the lion's share of the money while the girls just worked for the leftover crumbs.

Women's abuse was as old as time, men controlling women to do things, and make money off their bodies. Unfortunately, society never wanted to look upon the people who owned the women and the men who frequented them as real lawbreakers, only the women spent time in jail waiting to get bailed out by their pimp or madam. The working women always received the short end of the stick.

Chapter 55

It was four in the afternoon, and the new Dodger Stadium in Chavez Ravine looked pristine. The ballpark had only been open for two months when Mr. Lee and Armando Villalobos arrived in the four-door Lincoln Continental with its notable rear-hinged doors, which they had borrowed from General Lucian Richmond Hayes's garage in Indian Wells.

Armando exited the luxury car and stood looking over the vast parking area, the new Dodger building, and downtown Los Angeles in the distance. The late afternoon sky was clear, not the hint of a cloud, and the temperature had reached its crescendo at ninety-two degrees when the two men arrived.

Mr. Lee smiled. 'I understand tonight's game is a sellout, and the Chicago Cubs are in town.'

'Mr. Lee, you're correct on both counts. Do you want to go inside and watch batting practice?'

'No, Armando, I want us to wait here for the man we are meeting tonight.'

The two friends didn't have to wait long for their guest to arrive.

The man walked up and stood at the front of the Continental. He was lean at a five-feet- ten. The man's height was overshadowed by his complete confidence in himself. This was not a man one could slight or snub, and those who had taken him for granted were no longer among the living.

Mr. Kobayashi wore his thin hair flat to his left with a part on the right. He weighed one-hundred-thirty pounds, with brown eyes, round face, and a welcoming smile—to prove to onlookers this man was approachable.

Arata Kobayashi was interned at Manzanar, one of ten American internment camps for Japanese-Americans. Manzanar was the first concentration camp to deal with the Japanese problem; the internees arrived at the Owens Valley facility in mid-March

1942. More than eleven thousand were interred at its peak. 90 percent coming from the Los Angeles area. Mr. Kobayashi, wrenched out of law school halfway through his first year, turned twenty-two three months after arrival and joined the 442nd Regimental Combat Team in July 1942.

The 442nd Regimental Combat Team motto was, *Go for Broke.* They were also known as the Purple Heart Battalion. Kobayashi was wounded twice during the battle for the town of Castellina, Italy, in July 1944. After Italy, Kobayashi was part of the 442nd Regimental Combat Team, which was ordered to attempt the rescue of the Lost Battalion, two miles east of Biffontaine, in the Vosges area of Lorraine in northeastern France. It was there that he received his bronze oak leaf as a second Purple Heart of the war.

The war gave Mr. Kobayashi a reason to strive and prove to others he was not a second-class citizen. After his discharge at the end of the war, his drive lead him to graduate from Stanford Law in 1948, fifth in his class. He joined the Justice Department after graduation and became second in charge in the office of the United States Attorneys for the Central District of California.

Mr. Lee wasn't looking for Mr. Kobayashi when seeking assistance from the United States Attorney's Office in Los Angeles, but finding him was a godsend.

'I'm Mr. Kobayashi, Assistant United States Attorney for the Central District of California.'

'I'm Mr. Lee, and this is Armando Villalobos. We want to discuss the systematic executions of one hundred sixty-one Japanese men found at Furnace Creek in Death Valley.'

The men shook hands, and Mr. Kobayashi bowed slightly out of respect to the two older men and to let them know he regarded their news as noteworthy.

While the Dodgers held batting practice before their game against the Cubs, Armando and Mr. Lee told their story. All the details involved engaged the three men for more than an hour and a half.

Mr. Kobayashi only interrupted the narrative a few times to gather specific details.

The three men went into Dodger Stadium for the game between the Dodgers and the Cubs. Mr. Kobayashi's office had box seats along the third base side of the diamond. Dodger Dogs, roasted peanuts, and ice-cold beer completed the night, and the Dodgers, with Sandy Koufax on the mound, won.

###

The next day, Mr. Kobayashi discussed the information with his boss. They set up a group of twenty lawyers from the office and ten more from Washington, D.C., to organize a task force to apprehend and try the accused.

The Department of Justice was behind Mr. Kobayashi and the task force created in this case. No stone would be left unturned. The perpetrators and their accomplices were going to stand trial for the extermination of the men found in the burial site in Death Valley. The prosecution did not care about the reasons. There were no means to justify such ends.

Finding justice for the slain men buried at Furnace Creek quickly became a testament for the Assistant United States Attorney and the others in his task force. Murder was murder, but willful assassination was beyond the pale.

The Department of Justice kept the lid on the essensial facts of the mass murder of the Japanese in Death Valley. A Grand Jury was scheduled for the folowing week.

Chapter 56

A week after Mr. Lee and Armando Villalobos met with Arata Kobayashi, agents of the FBI, Army CID, and the sheriff's departments of Inyo and Riverside Counties were outside the mansion on the cul-de-sac of Desert Sky Trail. The place looked deserted at four in the morning.

Thirty law enforcement personnel were hunkered down behind vehicles down the street from the dark house. Seven FBI agents were stationed around the back of the house to make sure no individual escaped in that direction.

Red, Perry Rimmer, and I represented Inyo County. Our group walked up the cul-de-sac behind the FBI agents on the left side of the street. The Army CID agents and Riverside sheriff's personnel walked on the right of the road.

The night was still black, no light hinting over the mountains from the east. The temperature was cold in the desert, around forty degrees, and mist settled on sparse areas of grass in front of the house.

There was no light from inside the house. A message on a walkie-talkie told the lead FBI agent that his men were in place behind the house.

Conrad Palmer, the lead FBI agent, banged on the mahogany double front door. No sound came from inside. He hit again with no response. Palmer yelled out, 'This is the FBI, we have a search warrant. Open the door.'

Still no sound from inside. The last message from Mr. Kobayashi to Conrad Palmer, less than two hours before, stated that previous contact via Mr. Lee was two days ago. Mr. Lee told Mr. Kobayashi he was inside the residence with the two men who were to be arrested—First Sergeant Wade Arnold and Major Jamison Hayes.

Palmer turned around. 'Agent Evans, break down this door.'

Agent Evans lifted his leg and smashed his boot against the wood next to the doorknob. The wood split around the latch mechanism, and the door swung open into the foyer. FBI agents entered the building, shouting, 'FBI! Put your hands in the air!'

Several agents went down into the basement to search while others went upstairs.

My two deputies and I waited in the vestibule with Agent Palmer. A loud call for Agent Palmer came from the back of the house.

In the kitchen, two men were tied to wooden chairs with rope. Both individuals were covered in blood from multiple wounds. Their throats were slashed, and a sign hung with twine around each neck. The posters read: THIS IS WHAT HAPPENS TO TRAITORS.

The FBI took charge of the bodies. No one else was found in the mansion. The bedrooms, presumably used by Wade Arnold and Jamison Hayes, were in disarray.

Red, Perry Rimmer, and I went back to Inyo County. Three days later, a call came from the FBI in Los Angeles, positively identifying Mr. Lee and Armando Villalobos. The men had been killed twenty-four to thirty hours before the raid. A nationwide search was announced, centering on the missing Wade Arnold and Jamison Hayes.

Jamison Hayes no longer had any living relatives. Wade Arnold was never married and didn't have any relatives. Their pictures were plastered on all newspapers in California, Nevada, and Arizona. Television news covered the accused detailing their gruesome exploits from the Furnace Creek to the present, all the known dead, and asking the public for all information of the whereabouts of the two men. They were put on the FBI Most Wanted list, a distinction reserved for the worst of the worst criminals the FBI was hunting.

Hayes and Arnold were under a microscope, nowhere to turn, no safe harbor, alone, without any help from a fellow conspirator from their past life.

Chapter 57

'*Cabrón*, I want to know what the fuck you do when you go out alone.' Margarita stood frowning, with her arms crossed.

'Now, you want to know?' JB smiled. '*Mamacita*, you don't have to worry about what I do when I leave you for a few hours. I'm never with another woman.'

Margarita huffed. 'I know that for two reasons. First, if you were with some other woman, I'd cut off your *cojones*, and second, I'd kill you and the whore you were fucking.'

'Well, that would be a tall order. If I did fuck someone else, you'd never find out, and I would kill you before you had the chance.' JB smirked, taunting her. 'Killing mouthy women and stupid guys is something I've been doing since before you scratched your way into this world.'

'If that's the case, I want to go with you the next time, to learn how you do it, and then teach you a few tricks,' Margarita replied.

JB sneered at her. 'I don't need any help, and I forgot more than you will ever know.'

Margarita put her hands on his shoulders. 'Let me teach you what I do know, fucking men your age until you can't move anymore.'

Five hours later, the man stirred awake in the bed. He smelled *tacos al pastor*. He thought, this woman can fuck like no one else, and she can cook all that Mexican food like in a restaurant. He put on his underwear and walked out to the kitchen.

'I knew that I could wake you up if I made some *tacos al pastor*. *Cabrón*, you're the easiest man I've ever been with, in all my life.'

'Easy, how?' JB didn't like her mocking tone.

'I know what you like to eat and how you want to be fucked.' Margarita looked at him and smiled. 'Now, let's eat, and then we go out and find a couple of people to kill before we leave this place.'

JB smiled from ear to ear. He sat at the table, and Margarita set a plate before him. Guacamole and salsa were already on the table. He wolfed down two of the tacos and was starting on the third when Margarita sat on his lap. Her blouse was unbuttoned a couple of buttons from the top to show a hint of her breast.

'Like what you see, *Cabrón*?'

He looked up at her. 'Tonight will be the beginning of forever.'

Margarita got off his lap, holding his hand, and lead him back to the bedroom. Her smile said it all. This was going to be like taking candy from a baby.

By eleven that night, the couple had showered, put on clean clothes, and gone out to troll the bars in Palmdale, the next community south of Lancaster. They had packed all their belongings and tied the cardboard suitcases down to the bed of the truck.

Both were ready for the hunt. JB wore clean jeans and a blue long-sleeved shirt. Margarita wore heels with a pencil-style short skirt and an emerald green peasant blouse with three-quarter sleeves.

The couple went to a few Mexican bars in Palmdale, enjoying a few ice-cold bottles of Corona. Margarita was eyed by several Mexican men. She stirred a few hearts, and some *hombres* didn't like the gringo having his arm around her.

After the third bar, Margarita and JB walked out to the truck. He had his arm around her waist. They were laughing together when a man walked up from behind. This stranger grabbed JB's shoulder and pulled him around. Before either could talk, Margarita came up and looked the stranger in the face.

'Do you want me, *pendejo*, or do you want to fight the gringo?'

'I'll take you, *chica*.'

JB walked away and climbed into the truck.

The Mexican man put his arms around Margarita's waist as she put her arms around his neck. 'This what you want?'

'Yes, definitely, *chica*.'

She kissed him, taking him by surprise with her aggressive use of her tongue in his mouth. She put a hand on his crotch. The kiss broke, and the stranger smiled. Margarita still had her left arm around his neck. His smile faded; his body became limp.

Now Margarita had a smile on her face as she watched the man crumple to the ground in a heap. She took her knife from his abdomen, wiped the blood on his shirt, and laughed. Before kicking the corpse, she took all the money from his wallet, eighty-three dollars.

JB looked over at her. 'Does that feel better than fucking?'

Margarita reached over to rub her hand through JB's hair,. 'Almost, but you are the best, *Cabrón*. I want to get up on your lap for a ride.'

'Let's get out of this parking lot before someone comes out and puts two and two together with that body back there,' he replied.

'OK, but get there fast, I'm in no mood to wait, *entiende*!'

At three-thirty in the morning, JB and Margarita were traveling north of Lancaster, on Rte. 395 headed to Lone Pine.

At four, the Dodge truck was parked in the back of the Mt. Whitney Motel in Lone Pine, away from passing cars. JB registered for a room for a couple of nights. Margarita showered first after they dropped the suitcases on the floor. It was still dark when JB finally showered and crawled under the sheets. They slept until late the next afternoon.

They were exhausted from their trip to Palmdale and what followed in the parking lot. Margarita rode a contact high with the killing of the stranger, and JB found that watching his woman kill someone was almost as good as killing someone himself.

The two didn't dream; they had enough adrenaline to carry each to pure happiness.

Chapter 58

I arrived at the office early, before six, while the dew was still on the grass. The start of my day was looking over the information about any properties owned by Jamison Hayes, Lucian Richmond Hayes, and Wade Arnold, or their families.

The list had grown to more than thirty properties belonging to the Hayes family between Riverside, San Bernadine, and Inyo Counties. There was also a residence located in Los Angeles. All the properties out the United States were either sold or abandoned.

Wade Arnold didn't own any property. However, an aunt who'd passed away two years ago had lived in Keeler.

I decided that Perry Rimmer needed to sit down with Mrs. Haywood again. Mrs. Haywood, an eighty-year-old woman widow living in Keeler, an old zinc mining town east of Owens Lake, a friend of Perry Rimmer's uncle, Buster. Mrs. Haywood considered herself the town's resident news source.

I heard the front door open and looked up to see who'd come in so early. To my surprise, Edith Pearson walked into the station. She hung up her coat, put her handbag in the bottom drawer of her desk, and went to the breakroom.

I started going through the list of properties again, waiting for Edith to announce herself.

A few minutes later, Edith came into my office with two cups of coffee. She put one in front of me and then sat in the visitor's chair, in front of my desk. She leaned back into the seat, holding her cup in both hands in front of her.

'Good morning, Edith.' I took a sip of coffee. 'Mmm, just the way I like it. Thanks, Edith. If I didn't know you, I would say you're buttering up the boss. What's up?'

Edith leaned forward and took a deep breath. 'Jim, I'll get straight to the point. I'll need some time off in June. I've scheduled the Episcopalian Church for Saturday the twenty-third.

I've arranged with Juan Pérez to reserve The Western Bar and Restaurant for approximately fifty guests, from one in the afternoon to eight that night.' She paused a moment and smiled. 'And mostly, I need to know if you will walk me down the aisle for my wedding?'

This announcement came from so far out of left field that the ball was in the parking lot a second after it was hit for a home run. Not that I didn't want Edith to marry, but I was entirely caught off guard.

In my shock, I could only manage to say, 'Wha..?'

Edith looked at the ground and bit her lip, uncertainly. 'Well, Jim, what's your answer? Will you walk me down the aisle or not?' she asked quietly.

Sitting up straight in my chair and looking directly into her eyes, I grinned and replied, 'Yes, I would be honored to walk you down the aisle.'

Edith smiled and fell back into the chair.

I stood up and walked around my desk to embrace her.

'Edith, this is going to be the happiest day of your life. A new beginning with a man you love, I hope those tears signify joy.'

Smiling from ear to ear, Edith laughed. 'Oh, Jim, I feel like I'm in a dream. I couldn't be any happier.' She added, 'I'm a bit scared, but confident that, this time, I picked a good man. One who loves me and no one else. A man who wants to spend the rest of his life with only me.'

'So, who's the fortunate man?'

'Alex Morgan, you ninny!' She punched me in the shoulder. 'He's the man who came into my life with a ghastly discovery. He swept me off my feet in the blink of an eye.'

Edith twirled around and settled dramatically on the edge of my desk.

I was relieved to find out Alex Morgan is Edith's pick; I didn't want to say the wrong name and be stuck pulling my big left foot out of my mouth for the rest of my life.

I asked, 'Where is the honeymoon going to be?'

'Well...' Edith stopped and walked to the door, looking around. When she was sure no one was within hearing, she softly said, 'Jim, you can't tell anyone, but we've decided on a trip to Hawaii on a steamship. It's our little secret.'

'I won't tell a soul, except Conchita. How long do you need off for this adventure?'

'The trip will take two weeks.' Pausing, she asked, 'Is it doable?'

'Hmm...I think we can do it. Marlene is no longer here to gossip, so it should be doable.'

Edith sat down and sipped her coffee. 'Thank you, Jim.'

Changing the subject, I picked up some papers from my desk.

'I've been looking at the properties involved with Hayes and Arnold, and I want to look at anything Patrice Taggert and Scott Huddelson may have owned. I want to cover every base possible.'

Nodding, Edith replied, 'I'll get right on it.'

The telephone rang at the front desk and Marlene's replacement, the new receptionist, Georgia Scott, picked up. A few moments later, she buzzed me. 'Sheriff, I have the FBI from Los Angeles on the line.'

'Thanks, Georgia, I'll take it.' I pushed the button. 'This is Jim Cobb.'

'Sheriff, this is Mike Pryce with the FBI. I'm the lead agent on the Truck Killer case. He and his accomplice have hit again in Palmdale and Lancaster. A total of six murders in one night, four men and two women. It seems that the woman who has been riding with the assailant helped.'

I swallowed my anger. 'How were they killed?'

'Stabbed, and two different knives were used. Each victim was also robbed.'

Puzzled, I asked, 'How do you know that the killer was assisted by Margarita Gutiérrez?'

'Lipstick was found on the faces of two of the male victims.'

I rubbed my eyes. 'Unless you have her and her lipstick for a match, it's all circumstantial. I'd have the local officers canvas the stores that sell lipstick in the Mexican areas and see what the most popular color is. I'm sure the lipstick on the faces of the victims is the same color. Any witnesses?'

'No. At present, we have some people who think the people involved were the two we are looking for.'

'But nothing positive? Any other leads?' I asked hopefully.

'We canvased with the LA County Sheriff's Office and any other local law enforcement. No, witnesses, only hearsay.'

'Any idea where they are headed?' I asked, writing down the new information.

'The jurisdictions south of you, all the way to the border, are looking out for the Dodge truck. Nothing yet, also nothing from Los Angeles County or Kern County.' Mike paused for a moment. 'Ask your department to be hyper-vigilant in looking for these suspects.'

'I'll personally alert my deputies to scour the countywide. Have you contacted the CHP?'

'Yes, I talked with the substation in Bishop, and they will cover all the highways in your county. Other offices will cover the rest of California.'

'Thank you, Agent Pryce, I'll get this new information out to all my deputies, along with the description of the truck.'

Chapter 59

My deputies spent ten days looking at every structure in the county. Today, Red Fowler came in with good news. 'Jim, Bob Roth, and Carl Swanson found the Dodge truck in an underground storage area behind the Mt. Whitney Motel.'

'That's great, Red! Have a seat and tell me everything the boys found out.'

'Mr. Jay Polmar, you know him, the sixty-six-year-old recluse who owns the motel. Well, Jay told Bob and Carl that about two weeks ago, a scruffy, gruff-sounding guy with a scraggly three-day growth on his face came in early one morning, around five, driving the Dodge truck. He checked in for three days as a single, but after he left, the maids said he had a female companion in the room.'

'How did the maid know a woman was also in the room?' I asked.

'Female makeup products were left in the bathroom and in the wastebasket.'

I frowned. 'Did anyone see the woman?'

'No, but she could have been outside the room when the staff went in to freshen everything up.'

I knew the answer but had to ask. 'Any forwarding address after leaving?'

'No, Jim, but another fella came in the same afternoon the first guy came in and took the room next door. The second guy, Mr. Jerry Adams, is an encyclopedia salesman from Seattle on his way to Los Angeles. Adams drove in with a new 1962 Ford Fairlane, V-8, with four doors, the Town Sedan, in a dark blue metallic color. Ford calls it Chesapeake Blue.'

Nodding, I urged him to continue. 'What happened with Mr. Adams, Red?'

'Jay said Adams and his new car left the next day. The room key was still in the room. One of the maids said the bed wasn't slept in.'

'Did Bob or Carl do any follow-up on Mr. Adams?'

'Indeed. Mr. Adams never showed up in Los Angeles, and he is considered missing.' Red looked down at his notepad. 'His wife, Harriet, last heard from her husband the night before he checked in at the Mt. Whitney. Mr. Adams was at the Fitzgerald Hotel in Reno before driving down here.'

'Red, let's get back to the Dodge truck.'

'Yes, yes, of course, the truck.' Red flipped back a page. 'It was found in the underground garage that Jay Polmar hasn't used in at least five or six years. The hasp lock was broken off. All Jay can say is that it had to have happened since the guy in the Dodge truck signed in.'

'Did the guy in the truck sign his name in the register?'

Red gave me a half-smile. 'Yes, he did Jim, he signed in as Jack Baker.'

'Get forensics to go over the truck and tell everyone on the task force that the male suspect is using the name Jack Baker and contact the FBI. Also, tell them about the car Mr. Adams was driving. I think Mr. Baker is now the new owner of a Chesapeake Blue Ford Fairlane, a V8 with four doors.'

I paused, and Red said, 'The Town Sedan.' I smiled at Red for finishing my sentence. There never could be a better *segundo*.

'I'm on it, Jim.' Turning to leave, Red added, 'Oh, there's no news about the whereabouts of Jamison Hayes or Wade Arnold. Every house or property they, their relatives, or anyone they knew owned has been looked at, and nothing. All the property inside and outside the USA. We also checked any house linked with Scott Huddelson or Patrice Taggert, and anyone related to the two. Nothing.'

I said, 'Good work, Red, but Jamison Hayes or Wade Arnold are holed up somewhere. I think Scott Huddelson knows the answer. Is the wayward corporal talking?'

'No, Jim, Sam Ludo, and Carl Magnus have gone at him every way they can think of, and all they get is name, rank, and serial number. The son-of-a-bitch won't even talk with his army lawyer.'

I sat, still dumbfounded about the lack of communication from Scott Huddelson. A thought popped in my head. 'I think I know how to get Huddelson to talk. Ask Ludo and Magnus to come by the office tomorrow, and we can all sit down and discuss my offer.'

Chapter 60

The two most urgent cases I had right now were both equally frustrating.

The first case was the unknown man, now believed to be Jack Baker, and Margarita Gutiérrez, driving a new blue 1962 Ford Fairlane. We had to find these two killers, find the car, and then retrieve the body of Mr. Adams.

The second case involved who killed all those Japanese men and boys?

Where did the orders come from?

Why put them in Death Valley?

Why kill them at all?

And what about Jamison Hayes and Wade Arnold? Where were Hayes and Arnold hiding? Why? Who was helping them since the murders of Armando Villalobos and Mr. Lee?

I had come up with a plan to ferret out the whereabouts of the two retired military men. The lynchpin was Corporal Scott Huddelson. The unquestioning follower who carried out every order Major Hayes and First Sergeant Arnold dictated.

Huddelson obeyed each order without asking why. The man even killed his only living relative, his sister Patrice Taggert. Why kill Patrice?

Lastly, what kind of control do Hayes and Arnold have over Huddelson?

Ten o'clock found Carl Magnus, Sam Ludo, Red Fowler, Arata Kobayashi, and me in the conference room. We were joined by Hans Becker, the owner of the Wyman Bank of Palm Springs. Wyman Bank handled all the money and holdings of General Lucian Richmond Hayes.

I outlined the case details on the chalkboard.

~ *Who was responsible for the killing of 161 Japanese in Death Valley in 1942?*

~ *The three soldiers in the cave near Malpais Mesa*

~ Falsifying the deaths of Private Cox, Private Crenshaw, and Private Taylor

~ The fictitious death and burial of Scott Huddelson in France

~ The murder of Patrice Taggert

~ Murder of General Lucian Richmond Hayes and his house servant

~ Murders of Armando Villalobos and Mr. Lee

~ Location of all the landholdings of the Hayes Farm et al

After introducing everyone, I said, 'Mr. Becker, I'm interested in the last entry. We want your help.'

'Sheriff, Lucian Hayes was like an older brother when I grew up in the Coachella Valley; he taught me hunting and fishing. I idolized the man and his family. My father and Uncle Manfried opened the bank in 1882 after they immigrated from Germany. My family had been bankers in Hamburg since 1610.'

'That's all well and good, Mr. Becker. We all appreciate knowing about your family and the friendship you had with the general, but we are trying to find his son Jamison and Wade Arnold. We think that they are behind all the murders on the board. Do you know where they are?'

Mr. Becker was in utter shock when he learned about what Jameson Hayes and Wade Arnold did from Arata Kobayashi.

'Sheriff Cobb, Lucian Hayes had many secrets. He would use false names on deeds to keep his holding a secret. The man hated to pay taxes, and he didn't want anyone to know what he was doing or to whom.'

Arata Kobayashi asked, 'Mr. Becker, we aren't interested in Lucian Hayes's taxes or whatever secret dealings he had with other people in his life. The man is dead, and almost everyone he knew or had contact with is also gone. We are looking for his son Jamison and Jamison's sidekick, Wade Arnold. Can you help?'

Becker looked around the room at each man, seeing the need reflected in each, and he reluctantly said, 'Yes, I can try to help, Mr. Kobayashi.'

Over the next three hours, Mr. Becker divulged all the surreptitious dealings Lucian Hayes had within the United States and every other country in which he had holdings.

Becker's mind was a steel trap—he never forgot a thing. He suggested seven locations Jamison Hayes and Wade Arnold could be holed up in.

Mr. Becker left after relaying the information. I turned to everyone else in the room. 'What are we going to do about Scott Huddelson?'

'Hold him on a contempt charge and lock him in federal prison,' Arata Kobayashi insisted vehemently.

'I don't think he knows anything, anyway,' said Carl Magnus.

Sam Ludo added, 'Isn't he under arrest for the murder of his sister?'

'All the evidence points to him, but it is all circumstantial.' Red said. 'His sister, her house in China Lake, and her gun. Mrs. Fuller picked him out of a lineup. Huddelson can only be charged for the crime of assault and battery on Owen Snyder.'

'Gentlemen, I agree,' I put in, 'with all your insight and knowledge about Scott Huddelson. But what if we plant the idea that his two friends left the country, leaving him to take the load himself, alone.'

Magnus and Ludo asked simultaneously, 'What?'

'I'll go to Scott and say that we don't have a case about killing his sister. As an afterthought, I'll mention that the Major and First Sergeant Arnold were seen in San José, Costa Rica, two days ago, and that there is no extradition treaty between our two countries.'

There was grumbling among the men at the table for a minute. Mr. Kobayashi smiled. 'Let's give it a try, Jim, but with one proviso. We keep many eyes on Scott Huddelson. He may know where Hayes and Arnold are hiding, or he could lead us to wherever they hid their cash. He'll run if given a chance.'

Carl Magnus said, 'Let's bring some undercover FBI people from outside Southern California.'

'How long before they are in place?'

'Two days Jim, then have at it.'

My plan was going to find some purchase in the case now, if Huddelson took the bait. I needed to wait until the FBI undercover men were in place.

Chapter 61

'*C*hica, time to wake up. We need to be on the road before the sun rises.'

'I'm sleepy, and it's cold outside. I want to stay in bed. Come here and warm me up, then make passionate love to me, *cabrón*.'

'No, no, Chica! We must go before the cops find us. I found a place up past Bishop. A nice place we can hide out while everything cools down.'

'Okay, okay, *cabrón*, I'm awake.' She got up and went into the bathroom to take a shower.

A little more than an hour and a half later, the couple pulled up to the Sunshine Diner in Bishop. The sun hadn't risen over the mountains yet and the air was cold.

After breakfast, JB rolled a cigarette and lit it. Margarita slipped her right shoe off and rubbed her toes between his legs. They smiled at each other.

The waitress watching this escapade couldn't believe what was going on. She wanted the customers to leave this very minute, but her indignation subsided when the man asked for the check. She walked over to the table with the bill already written out. The waitress didn't ask if the diners wanted anything else. She just wanted them to go, preferably leaving a good-sized tip.

'Put your shoe back on, *chica;* it's time to go.'

Margarita did what was asked and turned to visit the restroom. JB went up to the counter and paid the bill, smiled at the waitress, and contemplated killing the bitch and taking all the money in the cash register. His smile widened when Margarita returned. She walked up to the man, threw her arms around his neck, and kissed him.

The waitress grunted, indignant at the public display.

Margarita rubbed lipstick off JB's lips. She then turned to the waitress and said, '*Pucera,* you know you want some of what I just got, but you're a dried-up *pucera,.*' The couple walked out.

The waitress didn't know what to say; she stuttered incoherently and wrung her hands, wanting to tear the Mexican woman's hair out. The waitress knew exactly what the woman had called her: pig. She had to sit down for a few minutes to make her heart stop racing, and her breathing return to normal.

Thirty minutes later, Sheriff's Deputy Perry Rimmer came in for his breakfast before checking into work. 'I'll have the regular, Wanda,' he said as he flipped the front page of the newspaper.

The waitress stood in front of Perry, not writing down the order.

Perry looked up, saw the look on the waitresses' face. 'What's wrong, Wanda?'

'I just served the most disgusting couple in my entire life. An old man and a young Mexican woman, who were grabbing each other in the booth and kissing as they paid the bill.'

The deputy sat up, suddenly alert. 'What did these people look like?'

'The man was forty-five or fifty, unkempt, wrinkled shirt, jeans, a dusty fedora, and a two-day-old beard.'

'How tall? What kind of build? Race?'

Confused, Wanda told him. 'Not tall, maybe five-ten, medium build, and he was one of us.'

'The woman, what about her?' Perry asked urgently.

'She was young, with a push-up bra under a shiny blouse, short skirt, black pumps, no stockings. The kind of woman you see hanging around on corners in L.A., or coming up to cars, showing themselves off. She wasn't...*decent.*'

'Wait, wait, Wanda, tell me more.' Perry pulled out his notepad. 'Did you see what they were driving?'

Still upset about the incident, Wanda raged on. 'They were revolting, touching each other like animals in front of the other customers. And the woman was a slut, saying the nastiest thing in Spanish to me.'

Perry tried to get her back on track. 'Wanda, what kind of car were they driving?'

'Huh? Oh, they took off in a new Ford sedan.' Wanda thought a moment. 'It was blue.'

'Wait, Wanda, I've got to call this into headquarters. Which way were they going?'

'It looked like they went north, Mammoth or Mono Lake, maybe Nevada. They were sickening. I don't know where they went.' Wanda shook her body, trying to rid herself of the memory of the customers. 'Ooh! I feel dirty, just talking about them. I can't even tell you what she called me. Disgusting!'

Perry went to the payphone in the vestibule of the diner, between the outside door and inner one into the restaurant.

Chapter 62

Perry Rimmer stood at the payphone in the vestibule of the Sunshine Diner.

'Hello, Georgia, this is Perry up in Bishop. I need to talk with Red Fowler. I think the man and the Mexican woman driving the stolen Ford Fairlane just left the diner.'

Georgia put Perry through to Red.

Perry relayed the information from Wanda.

Once he hung with Perry, Red told her, 'Georgia, get the Mono County Sheriff's Office on the phone, pronto.'

Red came into my office and repeated the information from Perry Rimmer.

The phone on my desk rang. 'Sheriff, I have the Mono County sheriff on the phone,' Georgia said.

I handed the phone to Red, who said, 'Sheriff Harper, this is Red Fowler from Inyo. I'm calling to inform you that the wanted man and young Mexican woman in a stolen new Ford Fairlane may be headed your way.'

We learned the Mono County Sheriff Department took the handoff from Inyo County and sent deputies from Bridgeport and set up a roadblock south of Lee Vining, preventing escape through Yosemite National Park and west into California's central valley. A patrol at Mammoth Lake set up a roadblock close to U. S. Route 395, stopping anyone from getting up into the mountain resort.

Perry Rimmer drove his police cruiser out to the junction of routes 395 and 6 just in case the killers tried to return to Bishop or go south. Red Fowler sent more deputies up to Bishop to reinforce Perry's position.

The sheriff's departments of Mono and Inyo Counties covered U. S. Route 395, the most likely road north. The only other road the man and Mexican woman could take was U. S. Route 6 north to Bento, California, in Mono County.

U. S. Route 6 meandered northeast from Bishop into wilderness territory before crossing the border with Nevada. Esmerelda County was listed as the second least-populated county in America, with fewer than six hundred people. Nye County, next to Esmerelda, had close to two thousand people.

Red Fowler called the sheriff's departments in both Nye and Esmerelda Counties in Nevada with information about the fugitive last seen in Bishop. If the criminals continued U.S. Route 6 east, then Tonopah was their destination, and the sheriff set up a roadblock west of town accordingly.

Red sent deputies out to California Route 266 at the Nevada border to set up a roadblock there in case the man and woman went south from U.S. Route 6 before getting to Tonopah.

Red also called the sheriff of Mineral County in Hawthorn. The Sheriff there agreed to set up a roadblock on Nevada State Route 360 / U.S. Route 95 south of Luning, cutting off any chance for the wanted criminals to drive north from U. S. Route 6.

'Jim, I've called the sheriffs in Nevada, and they are setting up roadblocks, in case this Margarita Gutiérrez and Jack Baker head east from Bishop into Nevada.' Red shook his head. 'It's a mighty big country out there, without nary a soul in sight.'

I told Red I also called the FBI. 'Now that everyone is on board, maybe we can catch these two before they kill again. Tell every man to keep their eyes open, and guns close, but only shoot if they need too.'

Maybe, just maybe, I thought, *one of the massive manhunts sitting on top of my desk was going to be resolved.* 'Maybe pigs can fly,' I said aloud.

Hope was all I had this day.

Chapter 63

A week had passed since the roadblocks were put up. The two Nevada counties moved their barricades to the California border and checked every dirt road and property for the Ford Fairlane. Mono County also moved their barriers to Inyo County and searched every house, barn, and road for the stolen car. My deputies went north from Bishop on U.S. Route 395 to Mono County.

The Ford Fairlane wasn't found. My men started to move up Rte. 6 out of Bishop to the Nevada line. Deputies came across what was thought to be a deserted house on a property that had gone into foreclosure.

The only person at the house was a young woman. My men used a cover story of searching for an abducted eight-year-old girl who had been missing for ten days. The woman said she was there alone, and that her *esposo* was in the central valley, picking walnuts. She claimed that they had been living on the property for the last four months.

I knew the woman was Margarita Gutiérrez. There were no other roads off Rte. 6 before crossing over into Nevada, so I requested that the roadblock there stay in place. I didn't want to set up anything south towards Bishop until we knew if the man was at the house. I had an idea he was hiding on the property. And the car we were looking for was in the barn.

I moved the roadblock to just north of Bishop and sent a team to set up a hunter's blind near the property in question to wait out the suspect.

As an officer of the law, I didn't care why this man, calling himself Jack Baker, did what he did, I just wanted to stop him. Permanently.

The standoff north of Bishop wasn't the only case on my plate; finding Jamison Hayes and Wade Arnold was another pressing matter. The most helpful bit of new information was the name of someone who had known Jamison Hayes his entire life—Nolan Dwyer.

Nolan Dwyer's family had arrived in Coachella Valley from Southampton, England, in 1890. Though flat broke when they arrived in Palm Springs, they soon met Lucian's father, Quency Malachi Hayes, an old friend of the Dwyer family from back home.

Aaron Dwyer worked for the Hayes family for the next sixty years. Nolan Dwyer was the son of Aaron and Moira's youngest boy.

Nolan and his two younger brothers grew up in Hayes' house. All three joined the California National Guard with Jamison Hayes in 1938. After the war, the two brothers moved to Northern California, while Nolan went to work for the Los Angeles County Sheriff's Department, where he still worked in the Lincoln Heights Jail in Los Angeles.

I drove down to the Lincoln Heights Jail without calling ahead. An ambush was the only way I could guarantee that he didn't prearrange what to say, or not be at work. I knew from my contacts in the sheriff's department that Nolan would be working before I arrived.

I waited in the warden's office of the jail, alone. When Nolan arrived, I introduced myself; we shook hands and sat down.

'What brings you down to Los Angeles, Sheriff?'

'I have some questions about your time in the military.' Watching him closely, I continued, 'I know that you joined the California National Guard in 1938 under Major Jamison Hayes.'

Dwyer smiled. 'Yes, I joined up as soon as he was commissioned and set up the Guard. The people knew the war was coming, and every able-bodied man in the Coachella Valley who knew the major wanted to be standing next to him.'

'When the war broke out, your unit went overseas and fought in Africa and Europe.'

Dwyer nodded, then explained, 'We went, but we were a headquarters company, to the rear of the fighting, but we sure wanted to be in the thick of things.'

'Did you go with Major Hayes and First Sergeant Wade Arnold on a field exercise in February 1942?'

Warily, he replied, 'The unit did field exercises all the time.'

'Did you round up Japanese men and execute them in Death Valley in February and March of 1942?'

Dwyer stood suddenly, knocking over his chair. 'What the fuck are you talking about?'

'Sergeant Dwyer, Corporal Scott Huddelson told me all about what you boys did to those Japanese men back then. The corporal is under arrest for his actions. Murder charges—he'll get cyanide at San Quintin for his actions.' I looked up at him. 'He stated that you were right alongside him during the executions in 1942.'

'Huddelson is a damn liar! I didn't do anything but round up those Japs in L.A. for Major Hayes. Those Japs bombed Pearl Harbor.' Looking at me defiantly, Dwyer stated, 'They all deserved death; it was a war.'

I frowned. 'Sergeant Dwyer, I want to stand up for a fellow law enforcement officer, but you have to be completely honest with me if you want to avoid the death penalty.'

At the thought of prison and possible execution, Nolan began to sweat.

'Now, Sergeant Dwyer, I want to hear the truth about what happened after Pearl Harbor and what the California National Guard did to those Japanese men and boys.'

I moved Dwyer to a small room down the hall from the warden's office. The little room had no windows, only a desk, and two chairs.

Over the next two hours, I heard the long and the short of what had happened. When some men balked—namely Cox, Crenshaw, and Taylor—to keep them from talking, they were killed by Wade Arnold, Scott Huddelson, and Nolan Dwyer. Nolan said his two brothers were never part of the round-up or killing of the Japanese.

Nolan told me the three dead soldiers were placed in the cave. They never went to Mexico. Dwyer insisted that he was just following orders. Doing what he always did for Major Hayes.

Nodding, I asked, 'How exactly were the three soldiers killed?'

'They were tied up and put in the back of a duce and half truck. I drove, and Scott guarded the prisoners. Wade Arnold drove the Jeep. Only the jeep could make it through the narrow trail to the cave.'

I watched Nolan form sweat on his upper lip as he paused in his story. The silence was deafening.

Nolan coughed and continued. 'Scott and I put the prisoners in the Jeep, and Arnold drove. Scott and I followed on foot. The trail was a good quarter of a mile long before the entrance to the cave. Wade backed in, and we put the three each in a seat, tied them down, Wade handed me a .22 revolver and told me to shoot each in the back of the head. We left the cave and walked back to the truck.'

I frowned. 'What happened to the revolver?'

'I handed it back to Arnold.'

The mystery seemed solved for now. I knew I would have a run at Nolan Dwyer once he was placed in the federal prison in Los Angeles.

My last question. 'Where are Jamison Hayes and Wade Arnold?'

'I don't know,' he said. There was panic in his eyes.

I shook my head. 'I'll ask again, where are Jamison Hayes and Wade Arnold?'

'Don't make me tell you, they will kill me.' Dwyer started to cry.

'Sergeant Dwyer, I need to know. Where are Hayes and Arnold hiding?'

Sobbing, Dwyer finally gave in. Speaking not much louder than a whisper, he told me where to find them. 'They're hiding out in a house I inherited from my parents, up in Keeler.'

The relief in the small interview room was palpable as I stood up and opened the door. Carl Magnus and Sam Ludo walked in. 'This is Agent Magnus of the FBI and Agent Sam Ludo of Army CID. Sergeant Nolan Dwyer, you are under arrest for the murders of one hundred sixty-one Japanese men in 1942.'

Dwyer looked around, confused. 'Sheriff, you said if I told you everything, I wouldn't go to jail.'

'I never said you wouldn't go to jail, I said that you might not receive the death penalty. At your trial, the court may take your cooperation into account when you are sentenced.'

Dwyer raised his voice in defiance. 'I was following orders! I didn't do anything other than follow orders!'

I shook my head. 'Mr. Dwyer, following orders was what the Nazi and Japanese officers claimed after the war, at the war crimes trials. They were all convicted and were hung or received long prison sentences. Following unlawful orders makes you complicit, not innocent.'

Magnus put handcuffs on Nolan Dwyer. The fate that awaited Dwyer in federal prison was something he wasn't going to be able to find protection from. The best thing for Dwyer would be solitary confinement, or the rabble in prison would eat him alive. Or they mght think he was a hero.

The FBI found Nolan Dwyer's two brothers up in Napa County. Under questioning, both admitted to following orders, as their older brother did. All the Dwyer brothers would be brought to trial.

Chapter 64

The ride back from the Lincoln Heights Jail gave me time to reflect. The sight of Nolan Dwyer, as the handcuffs closed over his wrists, made me feel like a win today was somehow achieved by breaking the rules. Nonetheless, one killer was going to jail, and the scourges who initiated all the terror on the unfortunate Japanese men in 1942 were still hiding out in Keller.

The next day, I sat down with the FBI, CID, and a United States attorney to discuss a plan to reconnoiter the area where the two suspects were hiding; we would map it out. We needed knowledge of the house and surrounding area, and a method for evaluating any civilians before assaulting the premises and arresting the suspects.

My only concern was making entirely sure that no harm came to the law enforcement officers involved in the takedown.

I had to push the arrest and siege planning to the back of my mind as I thought about another important event—the fifth birthday of our twin boys.

I walked in the front door a little after six. The dining room table was set for my family, my sister-in-law Rosita and her husband, and their children. I was glad to have arrived home before the cake was on the table and the candles lit.

My children greeted me with hugs and kisses, and my wife put her arms around me and whispered in my ear, 'I'm glad you made it home in time, or you would be the dead sheriff of Inyo County.'

Everyone sat around the table, Gabe and Tomas said grace together, and the feast began. I knew Conchita and Rosita had worked over the last week to make this meal memorable for the birthday boys. All their favorites were served, including chicken and pork enchiladas and refried beans. Plus their favorite—chocolate cake with chocolate ice cream.

The boys sat in the middle of the long table, each with his own chocolate cake. The candles were lit, and I turned the lights off. We sang "Happy Birthday" in English and Spanish before Gabe and Tomas blew out the candles.

Conchita and I gave the boys baseball gloves, a righty for Gabe, and a lefty for Tomas. Rosita and Pablo gave their nephews each a ball and bat, Rosie gave them baseball hats, Dodger blue with the L.A. insignia. The Dodgers had moved from Brooklyn to Los Angeles the year the twins were born.

This was the best birthday the boys ever had in their lives. I started to think about how we, as a family, could top this extravaganza next year.

A little past eleven, the party was over, and the kids were all asleep in their beds. The birthday boys clutched their baseball gloves while they slept.

I lay in bed, exhausted. It wasn't just the long drive to and from Los Angeles, the interrogation and arrest of Nolan Dwyer, and thinking about what I needed to do to capture Jamison Hayes and Wade Arnold. There was also Margarita Gutiérrez with her unknown man, possibly called Jack Baker. I wanted my brain to slow down.

Conchita came to bed and slipped under the covers. She put her hand on my chest and whispered softly in my ear, 'We are going to have another baby.'

I turned my head and looked at my adorable wife. 'I thought all through dinner, and the party, my wife, has a different face on; what is she up to?' I wrapped my arms around her, smiling. 'This is great news.'

We fell asleep in each other's arms, content with the news and happy for our family.

Chapter 65

The little community of Keeler, located on the east shore of Owens Lake, was south of Lone Pine off State Route 136. Three roads went into Keeler, but I knew that the house we sought stood on a dirt road off Laws Avenue, and there was only one way in and out of Laws Avenue.

The task force of ten men from the FBI and CID, plus Red Fowler and I, parked about twenty yards down the dirt road in front of Mrs. Haywood's house.

I knocked on her door and heard her shuffle slowly over to answer. 'Hold your damn horses, I'm coming.'

'Hello, Mrs. Haywood,' I greeted her. 'Remember me? Sheriff Cobb from Independence? I was out here a few weeks ago.'

'I'm old, Sheriff, but I'm not senile. Of course, I remember you coming out here with your deputy, Perry Rimmer.' Grinning, she waved me inside.

'I'm out here looking for a couple of men who are staying at a property belonging to Nolan Dwyer's parents. Do you know the house?'

'I do. It's a little bitty thing, two bedrooms and one bath.' She led me into the kitchen and took a pitcher of iced tea out of the refrigerator. 'The wife, Mary, raised the three boys alone, after she found out her husband was killed near the end of World War I. The kids all went to spend the winter vacation at the Hayes Date Farm down in Indian Wells.'

'Mrs. Haywood, do you know if there are two men at the Dwyer's old house?'

'Yes, of course, Sheriff. Major Jamison Hayes and First Sergeant Wade Arnold came up here about two weeks ago. They drove up in the kind of covered truck you see the military use, full of supplies.'

She paused a moment, pouring iced tea into glasses, and set one in front of me. 'One of the fellas from here, Hank Morton, helped them. Old Hank said they brought enough food for an army to stay more than a month and enough guns and ammunition to hold off all the Mexicans who stormed the Alamo.'

Shocked, I asked, 'Mrs. Haywood, why didn't you call my office about this information?'

'Well, now, Sheriff, I have those two under surveillance. I would have called if there was a change in plans. Buster and I know what they are doing every minute. They brought enough food and paraphernalia to live out their lives inside that little house.'

'What do you mean by *paraphernalia*, Mrs. Haywood?'

Leaning forward, she replied, 'A hospital bed came with the move-in. Hank told me. He also said that Major Hayes didn't look too good.'

The fiesty octogenarian knew precisely what she and her friend Buster were doing. I decided the better part of valor was to go along for the ride. There was no sense in fighting this fight. I took off my hat, rubbed my head, and sat down at the kitchen table.

'Mrs. Haywood, do you have a telephone?'

'Look here, Sheriff,' she leaned forward, hands planted firmly on the table. 'This may be a little bitty community, but we don't live in the dark ages. Yes, there is a phone.'

'Sorry, ma'am,' I said, nodding, 'I meant no offense. I'd like to use your telephone to call the Major, if that's okay?'

Smiling crookedly, Mrs. Haywood nodded.

'Thank you, ma'am, but first I have to talk with the other officers outside.'

I went outside and discussed the situation with Red Fowler, Carl Magnus, and Sam Ludo.

Mrs. Haywood let me back inside her house to call while the FBI and CID officers took up positions surrounding the Dwyer house.

The phone rang once before it was picked up. I said, 'This is Jim Cobb, Sheriff of Inyo County. Who's in charge?'

'This is First Sergeant Wade Arnold. What do you want, Sheriff?'

'First Sergeant, I came down to Indian Wells, and you and I talked at the Hayes date farm. I was looking for Major Hayes.'

'Yes, Sheriff.' He paused a moment before continuing. 'I said he was in Costa Rica at the property down there.'

'I remember our talk, but did the major return, and is he in the house with you now?'

The reply came slowly. 'He's returned, and yes, he is with me now.'

'I'm asking you to come out of the house with Major Hayes to talk with myself and agents from the FBI and CID.'

Wade laughed loudly into the phone. 'No can do. We are in the house, and we're not coming out.'

I leaned back in the chair and rubbed my forehead. 'First Sergeant Arnold, we know what you did and what you ordered your troops to do in Death Valley in 1942. We also know what you did to General Lucian Richmond Hayes and the man who worked for him, and we know about Armando Villalobos and Mr. Lee.' I continued, 'I'm asking you to come out and surrender and not let anyone else get hurt. There is no need for more bloodshed.'

'If you know about everything, then there isn't anything else to say,' came the terse reply.

'Sergeant, Nolan Dwyer confessed about everything you, Corporal Scott Huddelson, and the rest of the men in your command were ordered to do by Major Hayes.'

'Sheriff Cobb, there is nothing I can add to what you already know.' Wade sounded tired but determined. 'The major and I are soldiers. Whatever we did or ordered others to do was necessary for a time of war. We are still at war. We will never surrender. This conversation is ended.'

I was at a roadblock. The immovable object in the house was not budging. Hayes and Arnold were going to make a stand.

God only knew what type of weapons they had in the house. A frontal attack on the building could cause harm or death to some of the federal agents. I didn't know if the building was booby-trapped with explosives. There could be others in the building working with Hayes and Arnold. Or hostages.

The other question was how much food and water were already stored inside. A siege was a possibility, but not a good idea. News of this operation was sure to get out to the media, and all hell would break loose.

I wanted Major Hayes and First Sergeant Arnold alive to pay for their crimes. Hayes and Arnold wanted to go out in a blaze of glory for their horrific deeds. I remembered that in this type of a situation, getting the other side to change was near impossible, unless they had a reason. My determination led me to that goal.

I contemplated all the options available. Major Hayes and First Sergeant Arnold were going to die in the high desert area of my county. How many other law enforcement officers were to die would be up to debate; personally I hoped no one would have to die. The morality in me demanded that the evil in the house face the consequences of their actions. I wanted the world to know what a few egomaniacal men did for their warped sense of national honor.

Dammit, they needed to understand that no man was above the law.

I didn't want me, my men, and the other officers to sink to the unconscionable level Hayes and Arnold had sunk to.

Chapter 66

'*M*amacita, wake up. I will give you two choices, breakfast or sex. What is it going to be?'

Margarita pushed his hand away from her shoulder
and burrowed into her pillow.

'Wake up, woman, now.'

'*Cabrón*, let me sleep for a little while more, I'm tired. Give
me twenty minutes, and then I will make you breakfast or fuck
you, whatever you want.'

JB left the bedroom, and Margarita went back to sleep. Coffee was already made, so the man fixed a cup for himself, rolled
a cigarette, and walked out the back door to see the morning sky.

He sipped the coffee and took a deep drag on the cigarette
before flicking it off in the dust. Nothing moved; he was alone,
or so he thought.

Three hundred yards away, in a camouflaged six by ten-
foot structure, three deputies were up. They were looking at the
ranch house and the man standing out back by himself. Inside
the blind, there was a small Coleman propane camp stove. The
deputies drank coffee and watched the suspect.

'He slinked in with the pitch-black night, a little after one,'
Bob Roth informed Carl Swanson and Perry Rimmer before taking a slurp of fresh coffee. 'The fucker was so quiet, I didn't
realize he was there. He turned off the lights on the car before
entering the driveway and coasted into the barn. Didn't even
turn on a light in the house.'

'He must be antsy after being away for a couple of days. I
wonder where he went and how many he killed,' Carl said.

Bob replied, 'I'm sure news will come over the wire about his
latest exploits. May the dead rest in peace.'

Perry watched the man through binoculars. 'This guy is just
drinking his coffee and smoking, enjoying the morning. He must
think that he is God's gift to the free world.'

The back door opened, and Margarita stood in the doorway in satin short pajamas.

'Gentlemen, now this is a woman who wants some morning satisfaction,' Perry stated, thinking of his wife in bed alone in Bishop.

JB returned to the back porch, Margarita threw her arms around his neck and covered his mouth with hers. His hands rubbed her buttocks through the thin material of her pajamas. He picked her up, and she wrapped her legs around his waist. He walked back into the house through the open doorway.

JB lay his *mamacita* down on the bed.

'I guess we are not having breakfast,' she said.

Chapter 67

I stood outside Margaret Haywood's house in Keeler with Red, Carl Magnus, and Sam Ludo.

'I talked with Wade Arnold over the phone. He doesn't sound like he is interested in surrendering. He and Jamison Hayes have barricaded themselves in the house. I bet that they have enough food and water to last a good length of time, if we want to lay a siege. I also think they have enough firepower, automatic weapons, and maybe machine guns to hold off the agents we presently have here now. Any suggestions?'

'The FBI can bring in more agents and heavier firepower,' replied Carl.

Ludo added, 'The Army has some new types of grenades in their bag of tricks, concussion and tear gas, but I would bet these two assholes have gas masks.'

'There is also the problem of breaching the doors into the house; they may have set up tripwires and the like to blow up anyone trying to enter.' Red stopped and thought a moment. 'The houses out here don't have basements, but you never know if they dug one recently.'

I remembered the secret room under Patrice Taggert's house.

I nodded slowly. 'We definitely need some explosives experts out here for the doors, those grenades, and some more agents with heavy weapons. Let's get all we need out here by the end of the day and plan to attack in the morning,'

###

At four in the morning, Red and I arrived at an extensive assortment of men, vehicles, temporary living quarters, and searchlights. I knew the FBI and Army had gathered all the necessary elements, but I had one more ace I planned to play, before all hell broke out.

I watched FBI Agent Conrad Palmer drive up in a government car with a passenger.

I walked up to Palmer and his passenger. 'Good morning, Palmer, too early and too cold to ask you out here.'

'Yes, I agree about the time and the weather, Sheriff Cobb. Let me introduce you to Sofia Rios.'

Sofía Rios, a shy, beautiful young woman of sixteen, tall, with long raven black hair and piercing black eyes, an angled face and high cheek bones, straight white teeth, had a smile to disarm and casual observer. An innocent woman with a full life ahead of her.

I shook hands with Sofía. 'Let us go into the Command Tent and warm up a little.'

The tent was large and warm from several electric heaters run by a gas generator outside. We all took off our coats.

'Sofia, I'm happy that you made it out here to Keeler this early in the day. Did Agent Palmer explain everything to you on the ride?'

Looking around, unsure of what was going to happen, Sofia answered, 'Yes, he did, but I never met my father, and now that my mother was killed six months ago, I'm living with my *abuela* in Palm Springs. My mother never talked about the man who fathered me, but she told me that he wanted to marry her and move away from the Coachella Valley and Major Hayes.'

'Please, have a seat,' I said, leading her to some empty chairs. 'Did she ever say why it didn't happen?'

She sat down in the offered chair. 'Yes, Major Hayes was rich, and he said fucking non-whites was one thing, but marrying them was never going to happen to anyone in his command. The Major told Wade that Mexicans were dirty people, second class citizens, only good to do the work whites didn't want to do.'

'When was the last time your father visited your mother?'

'My mother told me he came around every few months in the beginning to visit her without Mr. Hayes knowing. I think my parents were very much in love. My mother said to me Wade Arnold was afraid if Hayes knew about the relationship, well... she said Hayes threatened to kill my mother and Wade.'

Sofia sat in her chair, frightened. 'He told my mother if she got pregnant, all three would die. When it happened, the final decision was agreed upon, my mother went to Mexicali across the border from Calexico to live with her oldest sister until I was born. My mother and Wade knew this was the only way to protect me from Hayes. Wade never came around to see my mother again, I don't think he ever saw me.'

I explained my game plan to Sofia, the FBI agents, Army CID agents, and Red. Everything was in place, if Wade Arnold didn't take my offer to come out of the house unarmed.

###

Mrs. Haywood, at eighty, had the vim and vigor of a woman of forty, still imbibing in her bourbon and Cohiba once a week, a trait she picked up from her father during World War I. This day she was drinking black coffee at five in the morning. She knew that something big was going to happen in her little town this morning.

'Sheriff, I don't mind the hullabaloo created in our corner of the world, but the quicker you get things done here, the better.'

I looked at the wise woman before me and realized I needed to come up with a plan to capture Jamison and Ward without making this a second gunfight at the O.K. Corral.

I went outside and walked around Mrs. Haywood's house. Trying to make all the players and parts mesh like cogs in giant machine. I got Sofía.

I went back inside Mrs. Haywood's house. 'I need to use your phone again.'

'Sure, sure, Sheriff. But who's this young woman?'

'Sofía Rios, meet Mrs. Haywood. Sofía is Wade Arnold's daughter.'

The two women shook hands but didn't say a word.

I knew I had some explaining to do, 'Wade Arnold knows she exists, but he doesn't know she is a girl.' At the look on Mrs. Haywood's face, I continued. 'Sofía's mother, Lupe Rios, never told Wade about Sofia's birth because she was afraid Jamison Hayes would kill them both, and Wade, too. Sofía was born in Mexicali, living with her aunts until high school, when she returned to Thermal and lived with her mother.'

Sofía began crying.

'Sheriff, that says a lot.' Mrs. Haywood took Sofía's hand and walked her to the back of the house and said, 'We girls need to talk over a few things alone.'

I called the house where Wade Arnold was barricaded in. It rang three times before he answered.

'First Sergeant Arnold, this is Sheriff Cobb; I have someone who would like to talk with you

'What the fuck?' Wade paused a moment. 'Who?'

I chose my words with care. 'Someone you will want to speak with.'

There was a silence on the line. I could imagine him considering his options, wondering what kind of trick I was playing.

Finally, he sighed. 'Okay, Sheriff, put whoever it is on the phone,'

I handed the phone to Sofia.

Nervously, she took it. 'Mr. Arnold, I don't know how to address you. My name is Sofia Rios, my mother was Lupe Rios.'

There was a moment of silence. Jim motioned with his hand for Sofía to keep talking.

'She was stabbed by a crazy man in a truck several months ago and died. My mother said that you and she were together after the war ended…and…um…I'm the result. I, uh, I just want you to know that I'm your daughter and…and I don't care what anyone has to say about it.'

Tears ran down her face as she struggled to speak. 'I don't want you to die today. I don't want to become an orphan before even saying hello. Please come out and meet me, *mi padre.*'

Listening, Sofía started to cry uncontrollably, wiping the tears from her face as she turned her back, away from Mrs. Haywood and me. She put the phone handset back in its cradle.

With her back to us, she sobbed. Mrs. Haywood went over and patted her shoulder and then took her into a hug. 'There now, child. It will all be all right. Come, sit, and have some tea.'

Tears were still running down her face when she turned to Mrs. Haywood. Nodding, she started to follow her. Stopping, she turned to me. 'My father wants to think about what I said,' she sobbed. 'He said to call him back in thirty minutes.'

Then Sofía followed Mrs. Haywood into the kitchen.

I didn't know what was going to happen, but the mere fact he was thinking about talking to his daughter was a step in the right direction.

Chapter 68

I timed it exactly. Sofía called back at the requested time.

While I waited for Sofía to talk to her dad in private, I stood outside the door and went over what I knew:

~ Jamison Hayes had lost his left arm in a traffic accident between his Jeep and a two-and-a-half-ton truck. The major's Jeep was hit broadside by the vehicle. The driver of the Jeep was killed instantly, while Hayes was thrown, landing under another vehicle driven by a French civilian.

~ First Sergeant Wade Arnold wrote a false incident report, claiming that the major's Jeep was attacked by the Germans. Major Hayes's arm was amputated at the time of the accident. Arnold made it sound as though Hayes fought off ten enemy soldiers while trying, unsuccessfully, to save his driver. Unfortunately for Wade Arnold, the officers who looked at the recommendation couldn't find any other corroborating information to award any commendation related to the accident.

~ A couple of days after the accident, General Lucian Hayes received news of his son's injuries and through his deep contacts with other General Staff Officers, was able to get First Sgt. Arnold to accompany Jamison to London and then return to Southern California in December 1944, for further recuperation. In all physical therapy lasted in London and at Hayes Date Ranch in Indian Wells.

~ The 275th Headquarters Company returned to Fort Irwin in late March 1945, including Corporal Scott Huddelson, Nolan Dwyer, and twenty others who had been with the company since its inception in California in 1938. The ten men who also served with the 275th Headquarters Company after joining the 4th Infantry Division of the Oklahoma National Guard all remained in Europe until the end of the war.

~ Wade Arnold stayed in touch with the remaining members of 275th Headquarters Company, and he instructed Nolan Dwyer to make a false death notice about Scott Huddelson with honors for heroism, plus burial in Europe.

~ The timing of the 275th Headquarters Company return coincided with the falsified deaths of Privates Cox, Crenshaw, and Taylor.

~ Corporal Scott Huddelson wanted his family to think he was dead and buried in Europe after the 45th Division crossed the Siegfried Line on March 17, 1944. The letter to Huddelson's mother, created and initiated by Wade Arnold, informed her that her beloved son perished in the line of duty and would be buried in France. The money sent at Christmastime helped the family endure the loss of a son and brother who lived less than two hundred miles away for the next twenty years.

~ A false burial in France was all Scott Huddelson wanted from Arnold and Hayes. Scott was never to see his family again after all the killing done in the name of the Major.

An hour passed before Sofía came outside. Her eyes were red, her nose was runny, and she looked wrung out. I stood with Red Fowler, Carl Magnus, and Sam Ludo, watching her become a butterfly after walking into the house as a cocoon.

'Sheriff Cobb, my father doesn't want Mr. Hayes's health jeopardized. He said the major had a stroke a couple of years ago and can't move his entire right side. My father doesn't want the man killed or hurt. He is…' She stopped and took a deep breath. 'He is willing to surrender.'

'Okay, Sofía. No one is going to die today.' I smiled. 'You did a great job.'

The next hour on the phone negotiating with Wade Arnold was taxing, exhausting, and successful.

Two ambulance attendants put Major Hayes on a gurney and loaded him into the ambulance. The frail-looking man was given oxygen, and an intravenous solution was started in his arm.

Sofía was able to spend an hour and a half with Wade Arnold, the father she had never met. Sofía shared her life story—growing up with her grandmother and then, as a teenager, with her mother. Not really knowing what her mother's job was. Sofía asked Lupe about her father but was told time and again she could never see him or know anything about him for her own safety. And his.

Wade Arnold listened to the tale, which ended with the tragedy of Lupe Rios' death. The Riverside County sheriff had called it a senseless killing by an unknown man driving a Chevy truck.

Wade Arnold and Sofía Rios gave each other an intense hug before saying goodbye. The FBI would take Arnold to Los Angeles for further interrogation. Arata Kobayashi would have a field day asking questions of Arnold.

I'd asked Carl Magnus if I could have some time with Wade Arnold before he was taken to Los Angeles. Arnold sat at the kitchen table in the house owned by Nolan Dwyer's family. Armed guards stood in each doorway, weapons at port arms.

Wade Arnold looked like all his get-up-and-go was gone.

I sat down at the table. 'Wade Arnold, I'm Sheriff Jim Cobb from Inyo County. Can I call you Wade?'

'Yes,' he said stoically.

'Wade, I would like you to start with the kidnapping and executions of the Japanese men in 1942.'

'It was war. The Japs attacked Pearl Harbor, we had to do something, the sneaky bastards couldn't get away with what they did to good white boys from America. Sheriff, you're American, you fought in the war, didn't ya?'

I nodded.

He continued, 'I'm sure you would have done the same thing Major Hayes ordered his men to do.'

I stared at him, disgusted. 'No, I wouldn't have followed an out-and-out treasonous order to kill innocent civilians, no matter who ordered it. America isn't like that, we don't kill people just to kill them, and we don't hide behind atrocities by using the excuse 'we were just following orders.' That's bullshit.'

'Think what you want, Sheriff, but war is war, and we were defending our country's honor.'

His twisted mindset sickened me. 'No, you weren't, Wade; you were following a delusional vendetta set by a deranged officer. If your version was true, you would not have had to hide it.'

Feeling my anger build, I pressed my palms into the table to keep from making fists. 'The Japanese-Americans who you executed were born in America. They were American citizens. They would have never worked with the Japanese in Japan.' Slowly, I continued, 'The volunteer soldiers from the internment camps, known as Nisei, most first-generation Americans, but not all; some had been born in Japan, became the 442nd Infantry Regiment. They were the most decorated soldiers in American Military History.'

Wade Arnold sneered but didn't respond.

Taking several deep breaths, I pulled myself together. 'Wade, explain the three men you killed and left in a cave in the Malpais Mesa area near Death Valley.'

'Those three fuckers refused to obey orders. They wanted to go outside the chain of command and report Major Hayes to the Adjutant General at Fort Irwin.' He paused, shrugged, and continued, 'There was a summary court-martial by Major Hayes. They were found guilty of treason, and they were executed for dereliction of duty during wartime.'

Confused, I asked, 'Then, why send their families false information about their deaths and burials in Europe?'

Wade smiled. 'That was my idea, to keep everything nice and tidy. What the families didn't know didn't hurt them. My way of telling the families was better than informing them that their sons were summarily court-martialed and executed. No, my way was the best way. We never thought the bodies would ever be found.'

'No, Wade, your way was a lie. The families now know their sons were executed in California. And sat in a Jeep in a cave for the last twenty years. If the families had an inkling of what happened, you and Major Hayes would have faced your own court-martial for treason.' I stared at him, then shook my head. 'Looks to me that you're just a twisted bigot who followed a bully into hell, killing innocent civilians. Murder is murder, no matter what you and Major Hayes wanted to call it.'

Wade Arnold smirked at my accusations and turned his head. 'Say what you want, Sheriff, but General Hayes had a lot of juice at the beginning of the war. He would have made us all heroes. There never would have been a court-martial.'

'Believe what you want, Wade. I talked with General Hayes, who said his son was dead to him before leaving California. I think the United States Attorney in Los Angeles will win his case against you and all the rest. The FBI is searching for any other soldiers who were with you in Death Valley. It is definitely a federal case, and the death penalty will be on the table.'

Wade Arnold's defiance drained away. His idol, Major Hayes, was no longer in charge, and Wade Arnold didn't know how to take over the charge up the hill in front of ememy fire.

'I have another question. Why kill General Hayes and his helper, Fernando, along with Armando Villalobos and Mr. Lee?'

'Huddelson killed the General and the pissant Filipino after he saw that you went to the house and talked. They were going to rat us out, so they had to go, like all traitors.'

Frowning, I thought about what Wade had said. Something didn't make sense to me. 'Why…' I paused, wondering if I really wanted the answer. 'Why did Huddelson kill his sister?'

'He hated her from before he could talk.' Wade shrugged. 'He didn't want me sending her any money, either. The boy was hardcore about his fucked-up family. A good soldier who followed orders, and kept his mouth shut, period.'

I rubbed my head. It ached from listening to Wade's sick words. Glancing at Wade, it occurs to me he might have the information I needed. I asked my next question, 'Was anyone else involved in the collection and killing of the Japanese-Americans, and the mass grave in Death Valley?'

Arnold rubbed his chin and thought hard and long on my question. I could see the wheels turning in his head; if he gave me names, would it help the feds go easier on him? Finally, he said, 'Come to recall, Sheriff, there was one other fellow involved. He even gave the Major and me the idea, A lawyer from Bishop.'

Leaning forward, I regarded him shrewdly. 'Name?'

'Donnie Turner.'

'Do you know if this Donnie Turner is still alive?'

'Yes, he is and doing well with cattle ranches in Colorado. He owns them but doesn't live there. He still lives in in Bishop. He shouldn't be hard to find.' He snickered and looked at me. 'He helped us, too. The Major made sure he couldn't turn on us. We offered to let him help us, and the fool jumped at the chance. Hell, we even let him kill all the Japs in Death Valley.' Wade Arnold had a smirk on his face after delivering this last bit of information.

I wasn't sure if this was Wade's attempt at a scapegoat. A mysterious man who 'gave' them the idea. It wouldn't save him. Their original idea or not, Wade and Hayes were the ones who took the idea, made it into a plan, and then followed through with it.

However, if there was someone out there, someone else who was willing to kill for their own twisted reasons, well, we would want to know what he was up to. We would have to do some checking into Donnie Turner, the lawyer from Bishop.

'One last question. Why so many?'

Arnold thought hard before he answered. 'You want to know? Sure, why not? The Major had a wife, her name was Ashley. Jamison met her in San Diego, with a bunch of other English high mucky-mucks when they came to Southern California. He had just turned twenty-nine, and the family was looking for a suitable wife for him. The General fixed it up, financially, with her family back in England.' Wade snorted. 'The fuckers stuck their little fingers out when they drank tea, but they were poor as church mice, living off dreams that weren't ever coming back. We all went to London for the wedding.'

He paused for a moment. 'She wasn't happy with the Major; he would get drunk and slap her around. He said it was his duty to control his wife. She went out and found an Oriental antiques dealer to spend Major Hayes's money on. Home decorating rage was Oriental, any kind. Mrs. Hayes filled the mansion up with all this lacquered stuff, dark red and black. The Major hated it. But he would do anything to keep his tight-assed wife. The Major didn't want anyone talking about his fucked-up marriage.'

I leaned back in my chair. 'Interesting story, but where does it go?'

Wade slammed his hand on the table.

'She *left* the Major for the Chinaman, that's where it goes! Can you imagine the Major's humiliation? Walked out, lock, stock and barrel! And he couldn't even get revenge because they hightailed it to England.'

I sat back in shock. 'So you're telling me he killed one-hundred sixty-one innocent Japanese men and boys in a blind rage because he couldn't get revenge on one Chinese man?'

'When you put it that way...' Wade muttered.

It was my turn to slam my hand down on the table. 'And you poor saps helped him because he convinced you it was all for patriotism!'

Finished with the interview, I left the kitchen, wanting to wash with a scrub brush to get Jamison Hayes and Wade Arnold out of my system. I glanced back and saw him put his head down on the table. Was he finally realizing he had thrown his life away? For worse than nothing.

I needed to get home to my wife and children. Look in their eyes and know that they represented all that was good and honest in America. The rest I had to file in a drawer that held evil and nothing else.

Chapter 69

The next morning outside Bishop, the air was crisp and fresh. California Rte. 6 north of Bishop had been quiet since my men waiting for the return of the man who drove first the Chevy, then the Dodge truck, and now the Ford Fairlane.

I was called when they realized the man had returned to the house.

My plan was simple—surround the house, drive up with a police cruiser, and use the loudspeaker to order the occupants to come out before storming the building. Simple, right, but simple is never that easy.

I'd brought up eight more deputies, ten FBI agents, including Carl Magnus, and had two patrol cars of the CHP sitting out on the highway blocking the long driveway from any suspects who might have escaped.

Before I left my house, I drank a cup of coffee with my wife, said I loved her and asked her to make some *pozole* soup with hominy and pork loin. Knowing Conchita, she started her soup before I got into the car, driven by Red Fowler.

It was turning light over the mountains to the east when Red and I parked thirty yards from the back door to the ranch house. Eight officers had surrounded the building and were hunkered down with shotguns, ready to advance.

Red and I crouched down behind the right rear of the car, and I spoke into the loudspeaker: 'This Sheriff Jim Cobb of the Inyo Sheriff's Office. The house is surrounded; come out with your hands up.'

The building was dead—not a sound, and no lights on inside, I let a couple of minutes pass. I picked up the loudspeaker again. 'Come out now, with your hands up.'

I signaled to the deputies. Perry turned the doorknob and kicked the door open. Bob Roth and Carl Swanson entered, one to the left and the other to the right, with Perry behind.

Carl came out of the kitchen door and stood on the back stoop. 'Jim, Red, come on in, everything is secured.'

Red, Carl, and I entered the kitchen. The house was deathly silent.

Perry called out, 'Come into the bedroom, Jim.'

There was blood everywhere. On the bed were two people. A woman, who could only be Margarita Gutiérrez, was naked under a thin sheet, and by the looks of the bruising around her neck, she was dead from strangulation. A scruffy man with a three-day-old beard, sitting up in the bed with his back to the headboard. He was holding his glistening intestines in his hands. Unbelievably, he was still alive.

'Carl, call for an ambulance, the coroner, and forensics.'

The man looked up and opened his eyes.

I bent down next to the bed and looked him in the eye. 'Mister, who are you, and what happened?'

He tried to speak; I bent closer to his mouth to listen.

'I'm Jack Baker, I think that you have been looking for me for a long time.'

'We have, Mr. Baker. What happened?'

'Margarita killed me this morning, with my own knife. She said I had killed one of the women she whored around with at the bar in Thermal, where I met her.' He snorted. 'Said the woman's name was Lupe Rios, her friend.' Closing his eyes, he grimaced in pain.

He coughed up some blood; it was becoming harder for Jack Baker to talk. Eventually, he caught his breath. 'I never knew Margarita was friends with this Lupe woman. I killed her just because she was available.'

I asked, 'What happened today?'

'I got back here, we fucked, drank some tequila. I was starting to fall asleep when I felt this pain in my gut.' He shook his head as if he couldn't believe it. 'I looked, and the bitch was slicing me up with my own knife. She looked me dead in the eyes and said, 'This is for Lupe Rios; you're a fucking excuse for a man, *cabrón*,' and she laughed, watching me die. Ah, but I have the last laugh, *mamacita*,' he said, his lip curling up in a snarl. 'I took her by the neck and squeezed her to death because I could, no fucking bitch is going to kill me...'

Baker's head dropped to his chest; I thought he was dead.

He looked up. 'I had to kill her, just because I could. Killing is what I do, because I wanted to take life whenever I wanted, fuck who, and when I wanted. I'm a free man, *gringo*.' He died with a smile on his lips.

The coroner took charge of the two deceased, shrouding them for transport to the funeral home. The county didn't have a full-time medical examiner. The arrangement was to take all bodies to the funeral home first before sending them to the medical examiner in Los Angeles. A forensic team from the lab in Sacramento worked on the house and barn. The car in the barn only showed prints from our killer, if he was indeed Jack Baker, and Jerry Adams. I doubted we would ever find his remains.

I needed to make one more phone call, to Sofía Rios; she would want to know that her mother's murder was avenged. And that the killer was dead at the hands of Margarita Gutiérrez, her mother's friend from Thermal. Poetic justice.

As I rode back to the office with Red, another idea presented itself. I would ask Conchita if Sofía Rios could come out and meet our family. The girl was going to become an orphan after the court, state or federal, had its way with Wade Arnold. Whatever time it took for the sentence to be rendered, I wanted Sofía to know us.

Sofía needed family in her life. She could join us.

The day after I saw Margarita Gutiérrez's dead body next to her killer, my family and I went to church. I said a prayer for Sofia and her mother, Lupe.

I wouldn't say any prayers for Wade Arnold or Jamison Hayes, may they be executed for their crimes.

Chapter 70

Red Fowler, FBI Agent Carl Magnus, Army CID Agent Sam Ludo, two deputies from my Department, and myself all drove from Independence to Bishop. There we met another FBI Agent and a CID Agents to join us on our visit to Donnie Turner at his house at 7 a.m. this brisk spring morning.

Wade Arnold had pointed the finger at Donnie Turner when I ask him if there was anyone else who helped in the massacre of Japanese Americans in Death Valley. Arnold said Turner helped kill all the Japanese. True? We were about to find out.

I had given Edith the task of researching Donnie Turner. She couldn't find much on him. His name was Donald Turner. His house, a Queen Anne Victorian, was built by his parents, Kenneth and Victoria Turner, back in the 1890s. Kenneth died from the flu pandemic in 1918, and Victoria passed away in 1950. His father made his fortune in silver. His mother was another one of those heiresses from England.

The only Turner left was Donnie, who graduated from Stanford Law in 1931. A lawyer who never practiced law a day in his life. Little else was known about him; he owned some property in Colorado, where he raised cattle, and a few parcels of land in the San Juaquin Valley near Fresno, where he had a table grape vineyard. There was no history of Donnie ever being married or any children, from information gathered from the family lawyers in Los Angeles.

The FBI Agent covered the back of the sprawling Victorian; CID watched the front. Red, Carl, Sam, and I walked up onto the porch. I pounded my fist on the thick, oak and cut-glass front door.

I called out, 'Inyo County Sherriff's Office, open up, we have a warrant.'

The house was dark, without any lights on. I banged again with the side of my fist.

The door opened, and a maid stood in the doorway. She looked older than Methuselah, her outfit was a wrinkled two-tone black and white affair. Her hair was in a bun, like a bird's nest, gray as the dawn on a gloomy day, her eyes were a tired corn silk blue, her body was slight, not more than a hundred pounds with thin arms, and she wore no makeup.

Her voice was harsh. 'What do you want, Sheriff?'

'I have a warrant to search the house and see Mr. Donnie Turner, ma'am, and who are you?'

'My name is Gertrude, Gertrude Abbot, I'm the chief cook and bottle washer hereabouts. I've been here since Donnie and Miss Victoria came home from the hospital.'

I didn't know what she was talking about. I showed her the warrant and asked, 'Is Mr. Turner home, Ms. Abbot?'

'I think he is still asleep. Come in and sit in the parlor, I'll go get him.'

'Thank you, ma'am.

Ms. Abbot ushered us into the parlor as she went up the stairs to inform Donnie Turner we were here.

The others sat in furniture which must have been brand new when the house was built; now it all looked like antiques. I walked around the room and looked at the paintings. I didn't know for sure, but the art looked like French impressionists—Van Gogh, Monet, Renoir, and Cézanne and the like. If my thinking was correct, then Turner's had a significant amount of worth in these paintings alone.

Ms. Abbot came back downstairs, looking confused, and said, 'Mr. Turner isn't upstairs. He and his clothes are gone.'

I said, 'Show me his room.'

I looked at the top of his dresser and found a handwritten note. I picked it and read: 'Sherriff, look in the desk drawer in my office downstairs, and you can read all about my exploits since I was a boy of twelve, through college, law school, and the years beyond. I'm sure you and others will enjoy my accomplishments.'

The room was cleaned out, nothing else belonging to Donnie Turner was left.

Red looked at me. 'What kind of ungodly shit did this asshole do?'

'Let's go see,' I replied.

We left the bedroom and headed downstairs. Ms. Abbot led us to Turner's office.

There we found several journals stating in detail all the murders which Donnie Turner had committed since 1918. He described each murder and animal mutilation down to the last detail. Every who, how, why, and the final resting place for each, when he knew a name, he gave it otherwise all the victims became Jane and John Doe.

Donnie described his grandfather and father's involvement with the Klan and private militias in Idaho and Nevada.

The mass execution was all his idea, and he told Hayes and Arnold how to accomplish the deed.

The tomes were sick and disheartening, how did someone get so off the usual path to perform what he did to innocent people and animals. Donnie's disregard for human life was astounding.

Turner's last note: 'Sorry, Sheriff, I could stick around for you to come and arrest me, but I'm just not cut out for prison. So, I must say *adieu* or *au revoir*. I decided to pack up my things and leave by the back door. I don't know where I will go, but I have a lot of money, and I will find happiness away from Inyo County.' A postscript stated, 'I don't think you, the military or the FBI will find me. Give my best to Hayes and Arnold before they are put to death at San Quentin.'

Ludo said, 'I guess with all this information, we can rule out where he didn't hideout.'

'I wouldn't take anything for granted. This killer could be anywhere, here or anyplace in the world. Happy hunting.' I looked at Ludo and Magnus.

Red Fowler interjected, 'This information is going to solve some extraordinarily old cold cases.'

Carl Magnus looked over and added, 'The FBI is interested in this information and the study of the human behavior of killers.'

Red nodded and walked out of the room.

I said, 'I hope the Bureau finds the answers for Donnie Turner's actions.' Counting the number of journals he filled, I figured we had a lot to go on. 'Thank God the man was a narcissist, and he wrote everything down.'

We continued looking through the rest of the office.

An hour later, Red came back into the office, 'I called the crime scene people to come.' He paused a moment. 'I also called a doctor to come to look at Ms. Abbot. He gave her something to calm her, but still, she's shaken. She did tell me that Victoria, his mother, is upstairs in an air-tight box. He embalmed her like the Egyptians, she is a mummy now.'

'Thanks, Red, I forgot about her. Poor woman, she never expected this.' Looking around the room, I said, 'the crime scene people can look at the rest of the house for any details as to what set Donnie Turner off down his trail of destruction.'

Sam Ludo just shook his head. 'The only entity getting anything out of this family is going to be the State of California. There will be no heirs, unless he left a will, giving all his money, holdings, paintings, and this house to a beneficiary.'

We all walked out of the sprawling house and into the morning sunshine. Looking back at the Turner home, it was hard to believe so much evil had lurked inside.

During the long ride back to Independence, I thought of my family and what my wife was making for *almuerzo*, lunch.

Acknowledgements

T hank you to Audrey Lintner of ALTO Editing Services for all the work performed for this novel. I also want to thank Jim Bilyeu, a retired Deputy of the Inyo County Sheriff's Department. No book is all one person's work, it takes many people to get to the finish line, my heartfelt thanks to my manuscript editor—Yvonne Blackstone from Blackstone editing. I want to thank my literary agent—Jan Kardys for her belief in myself and my work, and the co-agent from Black Hawk Literary Agency—Barbara Ellis.

Printed in the USA
CPSIA information can be obtained
at www.ICGtesting.com
LVHW012237170524
780605LV00001B/130